THE ASYLUM CONFESSIONS

FAMILY MATTERS

JACK STEEN

A huge shout out to Olin Lester.
I really appreciate all your help,
encouragement and advice!

For those who don't know -
Olin Lester is himself an author and you should check out his books on
Amazon.

NOTE TO READERS

You said you wanted more and so here it is! Actually, I've got about two other books that I'll work on after this.

Someone mentioned I should do themed books and that person was an absolute genius.

The theme of this book is all about the Family.

Then, there'll be one focused on the black widows who have been in my care. Both male and female. Black Widows are also known as Home Wreckers and that's exactly what these confessions focus on.

I also have enough confessions to go into a cult themed book. Yep, cult…as in satanic, alien shit and all that stuff. If you don't believe in satanists and witches and shit…these confessions might change your mind (that would be a good one to come out around Halloween, don't you think?).

I'll keep you in the look when they're close to being published.

A few things I'd like to say directly to you:

First - thank you for reading the first book and for picking this one up! Honestly, I figured this was a crap shoot and wasn't sure

if anyone would read these things. The fact you have, well...
you've made my day.

Second - keep those emails coming. So many have found me
on Facebook and sent me messages. That means a lot, seriously.
For the women trying to pick me up...appreciate the offers, I do,
but I'm good. And men, the same go for you - ha!

But those who email to tell me how much they've enjoyed the
confessions and asked their questions or shared their thoughts...
means a lot. Really, it does!

Now, onto the most important thing...every month I toast you
all down the at pub. Appreciate the support. Appreciate the beers.
Appreciate that you enjoy these confessions.

To my patients, to my new friends...salut!

WHO AM I?

My name is Jack Steen.

By now, if you've read a few of the other confessions, you recognize my name.

Just a reminder: I'm a nobody, really.

I'm not a writer. I'm not a storyteller. I'm not a goddamn thing.

I'm just a man working with those society wants to forget. I'm their companion into the afterlife, their death angel if you will. I give them the one thing they've been craving for since coming to the Asylum: an audience.

I work as a night nurse in the Asylum.

Which one? Doesn't matter - they're all the same. After you read the stories, you should be able to figure it out, but apparently, I might get sued if I say the name, so I won't.

So, what is it I do that's so special? Well, let me tell you: I take their deathbed confessions. The ones no one else has heard—the ones everyone wants to hear.

My patients tell me their stories, and they confess their messed up lives because I do what no one else in this fucking asylum does.

I listen.

I've worked here the longest out of anyone on my floor. I've got the scars, the stitches, the broken bones to prove it. I worked my way from the shittiest jobs here to the one I have now.

I used to think being a nurse was my calling. My passion.

I thought I could make a difference, that what I did was meaningful.

I was stupid to think anything in life was worth this shit.

I used to work in a hospital full of people who had lives and loved ones that cared about them. Most of my patients here have been discarded, forgotten about, left to spend their final days alone.

I won't tell you which hospital I work at.

I won't tell you the names of those dying.

But I won't lie to you.

You'll read exactly what I'm told.

The confessions you'll read here are all going to focus around one central theme. The first book were the confessions that left an impression on me, at least. The theme for this book will focus on the crazy dynamic we call family. I've got fathers and sons, mothers and daughters, brother versus brother and father and daughter.

Let me be honest - I don't have kids, none that I'm aware of at least. I'm a firm believer that just because you can father children, doesn't mean you should.

I'm also not going to tell you the names of my patients. But, if you're smart, if you can read between the lines, you'll know who is telling the story.

I can't say all the stories are one hundred percent true, but like every tale ever told, there's always a nugget of truth - but then, what the fuck do I know?

These sadistic bastards could be playing their final game with me by messing with my head, and now, they could be playing with yours.

A WORD OF WARNING

TO PREPARE YOU...

You're about to read four very different confessions.

Here's how the confessions go...once they're ready, I write down everything they say: their story and what they say to me, in between their storytelling.

Whether what they tell me is the honest truth, I'll leave that up to you to decide.

- Pops will never win the father of the year award.
- Farmer Joe is a smelly pig farmer and tried his best to be a good father but did a fucked up job of it.
- Henry likes to claim he's a mob boss.
- Mary only wanted to love all the babies in her care.

There will be more confessions coming, so if you like what you read, join my newsletter: Anytime I have a new book out, I'll send the newsletter, so you'll get 3-4 emails a year from me. Head to my website and sign up - www.jacksteenbooks.com or CLICK HERE FOR NEWSLETTER

Also...as one review said - I ain't no writer - just a night nurse. So if you're expecting writer-type stories, go read Stephen King (but read this one first...come on, give a guy a chance.)

Thanks for reading...

Jack Steen

POPS

PATIENT 424

CHAPTER
ONE

The quiet nights on the floor are my favorite. They're few and far between, so I enjoy them when I can.

Tonight is one of those nights.

We don't have many patients on the floor at the moment, which means I have no excuse not to get caught up on the paperwork that's piled about a mile high on my desk.

I might be exaggerating, but only a little. Paperwork is something I rarely enjoy doing.

To give you a little history: some of the patients who come on the floor stay for a long time; some hardly stay. I have a few long-term patients that feel like they have been here forever, their bodies on the brink of death, and yet, here they remain, stubborn to the end.

We may house the worst of the worst, the deplorable, the despicable, but death doesn't care who you are, what you've done, or how you've lived your life. Each patient under my care deserves to die with dignity, and I do my best to make sure they get it.

It's not always easy, though. I can't tell you the times I've had to talk to those I work with, reminding them that our patients don't need our judgments.

Tonight, Ike's sitting at the main desk, going over patient files while I'm doing some paperwork in the office. It's quiet, just as I like, until the phone rings.

Three minutes later, Ike's poking his head into my office.

"Incoming." One simple word, but it has me letting out a long sigh. I lean back in my chair, and cross my hands behind my neck.

"Which one?" We both glance over at the whiteboard on the wall. We've got a running list of inmates we're expecting to come to the floor.

"The one at the top."

About time. I've been waiting for this one to arrive for a few weeks now. The incoming patient, we'll call him…Pops.

Pops has been an inmate of The Asylum for forty or so years. When he came, he had some socializing issues and had to be segregated for his own safety. Eventually, the others became more accepting of his presence and even look to him as a father figure now.

"Let's put him in room 8. The floors were just washed in there."

Ike gives a salute before closing the door behind him. While he's getting the room ready for Pops, I need to get a file prepared for him.

He's got a red star beside his name on the whiteboard. A red star means I want his confession, so I'm looking forward to spending some quality time with Pops when he's ready.

He's one of the few I've been wanting his confession for a while now. I know in my bones that he's never told the full truth of what he's done.

Now, I'm not a father, never had a kid of my own, so relating to Pops might be challenging. I doubt I'll ever understand the reasoning behind what he did, and to be honest, it grosses me out.

You're wanting to know his story now, don't you?

Let me just say this: Pops was a dedicated father, and in his eyes, no one was worthy of his daughter's heart. No one but him and anyone who tried to steal his daughter's heart…he killed them.

CHAPTER
TWO

I'm standing in the hallway as the elevator door opens. Two guards push a bed through the open doors and head toward me.

Pops is lying there, holding on to a saline bag, surrounded by his few possessions. His eyes remain closed, but as he comes my way, I see there's a smile on his face.

What's he got to smile about?

"Waiting for me, are you?" Pops' gravely voice greets me as he opens one eye.

"Took your time, old man." The welcome is in my voice, and I know he hears it.

"Got tired of waiting for you to come check on me. Figured it," Pops stops as he struggles to catch his breath. His lungs aren't doing too good, and I hear it plain as day. "Figured it was time I come to you instead."

I walk along beside him as the guards push him toward his room. Ike stands at the door, waiting. I take Pops' hand and give it a soft shake.

"I made you a promise a few years ago, remember?" I say.

He opens one eye, then closes it. "Sure do."

There's an area in the back gardens where some inmates like to hang out and smoke. Sometimes I go down to join them. I'm not much of a smoker, but it's more for the company and to get a feel for where people are at.

I want most of my future patients to know who I am before they come to my floor.

A few years ago, I'd sat with Pops at the picnic table. He shared stories from his life before, telling tales I'm sure, of what a great guy he was. By the time we were alone, my break was almost up. Pops looked up at me when I stood and asked if I'd be joining him again next shift. I thought about it, I really did, but I knew the show he'd put on had been for my benefit. So I told him no. I told him the next time he saw me, he'd be coming to me, tired of living his lie and ready to tell the truth. He asked if that was a promise or a threat. I told him it was a promise.

A promise I've been sure to keep.

"Ike here is going to get you set up in your room and make sure you're taken care of. I'll be in to see you later." I give the bed bars a slap before stepping away.

I've been going over Pops' file, wanting to familiarize myself with his medical history as well as read the notes his guards and doctors wrote down.

He's quite the fellow. Friendly when he wants to be. Scary when he needs to be. Multiple times I've read casual warnings from guards to not turn your back to him when he's in a mood, and you could always tell his mood by how quiet he became.

I guess a quiet Pops is a dangerous Pops.

Before heading back downstairs, there's a knock on the door.

It's one of the guards from Pops floor.

"Hey, Swiggy. It's been a while," I say. I'm in the middle of pouring two shots of Scotch into a glass. I figured Swiggy would come to join me.

"None for me. The missus and I are doing a dry month."

I set his glass to the side, down mine, and then lean against my desk.

"This is a shitty month to be going dry." I can't imagine doing that.

"Yeah, well, she thinks I'm drinking too much and asked me to lay off it for a bit. I can't say no to her, so here I am. Hey, I wanted to ask, where have you gotten to lately? Keep thinking I'll see you downstairs during breaks, but you never come."

I point to the stack of boxes in the corner of my small office. "The Warden gave me a deadline to go through a bunch of files and clean them up. If I get them done before his deadline, there's a bottle of top-shelf bourbon with my name on it."

"Sweet. He doesn't give away his bourbon too often. I hope you get it. Listen," he pauses, glancing over his shoulder. "There's something you need to know about Pops."

He's got a look on his face, one I'm having a hard time reading, and I've known Swiggy a hell of a long time.

"His daughter came to visit, first time since he came here."

This news doesn't surprise me. Pops isn't the first inmate to go without familial visitors. Some families find it too difficult to visit; some are ashamed, embarrassed, and prefer to walk different paths with the past behind them.

"How did this affect our new patient?"

Swiggy lets out a long sigh. "That's when his health went downhill."

I don't like the sound of that.

"Do you know what happened between the two of them?"

Swiggy shakes his head. "Figured you could use your magic and get it out of him."

Of course, he does.

"When was she here?"

"Two weeks ago."

It always surprises me what it takes for men to give up. Some decide on their own, some have it decided for them. I wonder which was it for Pops? Did something happen? Were things said that couldn't be taken back? Something broke him, that's for sure.

CHAPTER
THREE

Pops is waiting for me as I enter his room, his face empty of all emotion but one.

Sadness.

"Well, Old Man, I certainly didn't expect to see you so soon."

Ike set up Pops' room to make it as comfy as he could. The meal tray is full of his few belongings, an extra blanket was added to cover his legs, and even the pillow looks puffed.

Guess Ike likes Pops, which is surprising because Ike doesn't like many of our patients.

"Anything I can get for you? Fresh steak? Chocolate sundae?" I make sure he sees the smile, hears the laughter in my voice. It's nice when I see him return my smile.

I check on his IV, making sure everything as it should be.

"Fuck off, Jack." It's a mumble, more of a grumble, but I hear him loud and clear.

I search for a cup, fill it with water, and then bring it close to his lips, making sure to add a straw. "Slowly, slowly," I say as he sips the water.

His lips are chapped, his skin is dry, and it pisses me off that no one would have taken care of this before sending him up here. Death with dignity isn't a complex concept to grasp.

"Any beer? Or something harder?" He asks after I take the cup away.

I snort. Like I'm going to share the little I keep stashed away with him.

"Oh come on," he says. "Surely you can spare a little for a dying man. Especially if it's my last wish, right?"

"I'll give you a last wish, but I guarantee it won't be for a drink." I push my shoulders back and enjoy the loud cracking sound that accompanies my stretch.

Pops looks at me, staring with a question in his gaze. It's a look I'm familiar with, a question he knows I can answer.

"You want an answer, you're going to have to ask the question," I say, being a hard ass.

He twists his head so he's looking at the bare wall instead of me. What does he hope to see there?

I give another stretch, releasing a sigh as I do so.

This seems to grab his attention.

"I'm dying," he says.

I reach for his chart and flip through it. "Appears so. Did you finally decide it was time?"

This grabs his attention. He slowly turns his head back my way.

"Turns out I was holding on to something that was never there." I hear everything he doesn't say in his tone. The heartbreak is real.

"Worth dying for, though?"

"Not worth living for, that's damn sure." His eyes close, and I see the defeat that's there, on his face, flowing through his blood.

I rest my hand on his shoulder, giving a slight squeeze.

"I've got rounds to do, but I'll check in on you later, okay?" I'm surprised he hasn't asked the question yet.

Just as I'm about to close his door behind me, he says the words: "I hear you make deals."

I pause, give it a moment, then return to his side.

"Depends on the deal."

"Story for a deal?" There's a glimmer in his eyes, like he's enjoying this give and take between us.

"I like stories. Is it a real or…"

He nods. "It's real. I heard you like the ones no one else has heard. That true?"

I lift a shoulder in a shrug. "You've got one to tell?"

His eyes close for a second, and when he reopens them, I can see all the fight is gone.

Pops isn't going to last long. Death is there, waiting. I can feel it's presence in the room, the chill that swirls around my ankles.

I decide to make this easy on him. "What are you scared of the most?" I ask.

Nine times out of ten, when I ask this question, the answer is always death. They're afraid of the act of death, of what it's like in those last few seconds.

"Dying. Alone." Pops says. "I don't care what happens after. I've already lived through hell. I just don't want to greet the end by myself, you know?"

He's surprised me, I'll say that much. Ultimately though, I understand this fear more than most.

I, too, don't want to die alone.

"You tell me your story, the real one, the one you haven't told yet, and I'll be here, with you, till the end." I hold my hand out, waiting to see if he'll find the energy to grab hold of it.

It takes some time, but he does.

"Deal."

CHAPTER
FOUR

POPS TO JACK

I'm not afraid of Death, Jack.

Death isn't scary. It's not the end either, no matter what people say.

Death has been here, with me, for the past few days. It whispers to me, did you know? The voice has a melody to it - it's not cold or harsh. It's actually quite soothing. I guess the melody depends on who you are, though, right?

What would you hear if Death were beside you, whispering to you?

I think Death has many faces, many voices, and it all depends on the person you are, and what you've done with your life.

What do you believe, Jack? You still haven't answered me...what voice do you think you'll hear when it's your time?

Fine, this is about me, not you.

Do me a favor? I know you've got a bottle of Scotch in your office; you let it slip a long time ago that you like to keep one handy. I'm sure you pour yourself a glass when one of us dies, am I right?

Will you pour it now? Bring it in here? Not for me to drink, but to smell? I'd like to leave with that memory, if I can. I find Scotch has the pour to burn away the pain, if you know what I mean.

No? Will you at least give me more pain meds to dull the deep ache in my bones and slow the rush of fire in my veins?

Ahh…thank you.

Do you have children, Jack? Have you ever wanted any?

They are our greatest comfort, our strongest joy, and our bitter disaster.

I have a story.

It'll be my last one.

It's a story I never thought I'd need to tell, because I never thought I'd be alone.

Being alone has always been my greatest fear. Funny how those fears manifest when Death arrives, isn't it?

CHAPTER
FIVE

POPS

I grew in a large family. I was the middle child, the forgotten child. I was raised by my brothers and sisters, surrounded by chaos, and never knew a moment of peace.

I was never alone, though. I never knew what it was to live in a quiet house, where peace reigned. I grew up only knowing hardship, how to fight, how to protect, and how to keep what I had.

It was a good life. Not an easy one - but, a good one.

I fell in love at an early age. Mary Beth Summers. She was my everything, my fairy tale in the making, and I grew up worshiping the ground she walked on. I was only twelve, but I knew that Mary Beth Summers was the only one for me as soon as she gave me a black eye.

We married, and moved into a small one story cabin home on the back of her parents farm land. Her daddy was a crop farmer and I'd help him as needed. We laid claim to the small area around us, with Mary Beth planting a garden, and I built us a chicken coop. We both dreamed of filling our home with unruly children.

We were married ten years. They weren't easy years and we

learned what it meant to survive through loss. Mary Beth lost both of her parents and we lost many children before they were born. I threw myself into my work, building a name for myself as a mechanic, instead of dealing with the grief that filled my home.

I could have done better. I should have done better. I loved my wife but I lost myself in grief, not realizing she was just as lost as I was.

A miracle happened shortly after our tenth wedding anniversary. We had a little baby girl, the most beautiful tiny being I couldn't believe was mine.

Mary Beth though, while I held our baby, she lay in that bed of ours and died. The birth was too much for her.

I never understood heartache until the moment when I realized she was gone. I never understood what it truly meant to live without Mary Beth until I had no choice but to do so. It was the hardest thing I've ever done in my life...until now.

I was a widower with a daughter to raise, and if it weren't for my sisters who came to help me with her, we both would have been lost.

As it was, she ended up being my Angel, my savior.

I used to love it when she'd fall asleep on my chest, her tiny body against mine. I still remember that first smile of hers - so innocent, so peaceful. I made her a promise then, to always see a smile on her face, to always protect her innocence, to always keep her safe.

It was a promise made by a father. A promise I always intended to keep.

My youngest sister came to live with me until Angel was old enough to go to school. Then, it was just her and me, and the bond between us was strong.

She was my shadow. When she wasn't in school, she was with me in the garage, getting her hands dirty, understanding the pride that comes with working with your hands, using your brain and skills to fix what is broken.

She built her first motorcycle all on her own. She worked in her mother's garden. She knew how to hunt. Angel was everything I'd wanted in a child, and I couldn't have been more proud.

I am still so very proud. Even now, even when it hurts to be so.

I loved having her as my little shadow. The thing about shadows, though, they don't always stay in one place.

The same could be said about children. While they remain young, it's easy to lead them, direct them, and teach them but eventually, children get to a point where they want to lead themselves, go in their own directions, and seek out guidance by others than the one who raised them.

My parents warned me that it wouldn't be easy raising a child. I should have listened.

Angel never disobeyed me. Until she did.

She never went against my word. Until she did.

She always heeded my advice. Until she stopped listening.

Just because a child decides they want to be treated as an adult doesn't mean they are ready for adulthood.

My job, as her father, was to realize this and keep her safe, even if from herself.

She always had friends, boys, girls; they were one and the same back then. At a certain age though, I noticed her friendships started changing. Fewer girls hung around, and more and more boys started showing up.

Here's the thing: As her father, I was okay with the boys until I noticed them looking at her differently. I recognized those looks, understood those looks, and I didn't like them.

Soon Angel and I started fighting, as most parents would understand. She felt I was being too...protective. I thought she was being too...free. I didn't like how the boys would hang around, always there, always watching my daughter.

If she wasn't going to protect her honor, I would have to. That's the way it is with fathers and daughters.

I would sit out on the front porch at night, cleaning my gun, being a Neanderthal, as Angel would say. I made sure the boys knew I was comfortable with guns. Sometimes I'd ask them to come hunting with me. Only a few ever took me up on the offer.

Few walked away unscathed.

I'd offer to take a look at their cars or trucks, give them a once over, and during those checkups, I'd make it very clear my intentions if they ever placed my daughter in a compromising situation.

At first, my threats worked. The boys would show respect for both myself and Angel when they came around. They listened to my words, made sure she was home by curfew, that sort of thing.

Eventually, though, the threats stopped working. That's when I invited the first boy to come hunting with me, just the two of us.

The stupid boy got in the way of a shot, and his shoulder bore the price. I bandaged him up, made sure he made it to the hospital, but that was the last we saw of him. His mother tried to have some words with me, but his own father understood the rules of the hunt.

The next boy I invited to come hunting with me declined. He thought he was being clever, but he was using the wrong head to think with if you know what I mean. I caught him sneaking around the yard late at night after fooling around with my daughter.

He didn't make it home that night, and his body was found back in the woods, half mauled by wolves.

I'm not saying I had anything to do with helping those wolves sniff out the scent of blood, but the kid was stupid enough to think he could hunt my daughter on my property...

What kind of father would I be if I didn't protect my daughter's honor?

CHAPTER
SIX

POPS TO JACK

Ahhh, you've heard that story before, have you? I'm not surprised, they hinted at it during my trial, but it could never be proved.

Well, let me make it clear, Jack. That boy never saw me coming.

I knew the wolves were in the fields behind my house, I'd heard them for the past two nights, howling at the moon, warning everyone they were in the area.

I don't have a spirit animal, but if I did, it would be the wolf. A wolf knows how to protect his own, and it doesn't matter who gets in the way.

Every father should love his daughter like that, don't you think?

She was my everything. As a man, I knew those boys only saw her as one thing, and there was no way in hell they would ever get a taste of her.

My love for her was pure. I don't care how the lawyers and media painted me, I don't care what they say I did or didn't do to my daughter. I loved her, I protected her, and I did everything I could to keep her safe.

Are you going to vilify me, like everyone else, for loving her?

Yes, I held her in my arms.

Yes, I kissed her.

Yes, I knew her as my own because she was.

She was of my blood, of my flesh.

Let me be clear about something: I never defiled her. Never took or forced her love.

I'm not a monster, Jack. No matter what people may say.

Angel and I, we had a different bond than most parents do with their children. She was my everything.

When she was little, she would crawl into my bed in the dead of night and ask me to tell her stories of Mommy. She said she always felt safe with me. How is that wrong? How is that evil?

Yes, of course, there comes a point when a woman's body becomes her own and not her parents. I respected that, as any father would and should.

Let me make it very clear. I never took what was never mine to take. Angel, she gave me her love, freely, innocently, as a daughter should to her father.

I never abused that trust. I don't care what anyone else says.

They're just sick fucks. I killed people, yes. But I never raped my daughter. Never.

CHAPTER
SEVEN

POPS

If there's something my daughter is not - it's stupid.

She takes after both her mother and me. She was heartbroken when that boy's body was recovered in the forest. We both went to the funeral, closed casket, and I held her close as her tears ran non-stop.

The minute we arrived home, she offered to make dinner while I worked on a car out in the garage.

I didn't think anything of it, why would I? We often alternated making dinner, and it was nice of her to take care of it.

When she called me into the house, there were two dishes in front of where I sat.

She asked me if I loved her.

She asked me if I trusted her.

Both times, I answered yes.

She then told me that one dish had been poisoned but wouldn't tell me which one.

Now, a sane man would have tossed both of the dishes into the garbage and punished the girl for attempting to kill me.

I've never claimed to be sane. Not then, and sure as hell not now.

I asked her why she would want to kill me, her own father, and her answer was simple.

For the same reason, I go out of my way to keep her safe and protected: because she loved me.

Again, a sane man wouldn't have understood her reasoning.

Do you, Jack?

Probably not.

But I did, and I still do.

So, I did the only thing I could. I pulled both of the dishes close, and one fork at a time, I took bites out of both, always watching for my daughter's reaction, never taking my eyes off of her.

She wore a mask of indifference. It didn't matter which plate I ate from, the expression on her face remained the same.

See…I knew my daughter. I knew she would never hurt me. I knew she'd never poisoned me.

I knew she'd lied about trying to kill me.

She got her message across, all the same, not that it mattered.

The next boy that showed interest in her…she didn't invite him back to the house, she didn't introduce us or even tell me she was dating someone. I found out the way most parents do, I guess…by snooping.

My youngest sister, when she still lived with us, encouraged Angel to keep a diary. Every year on her birthday, my sister would gift her a new journal, one to fill up the pages with her thoughts and dreams.

For the longest time, I gave her privacy and never read the diary.

But when she started to hide things from me, I had no choice. I needed to know her secrets so I could fulfill those promises I'd made at her birth.

Girls are fanciful creatures. The thoughts and feelings they experience daily would be exhausting for us men. I remember when my wife would write me love letters, the passion she'd pour into those notes humbled me, and my daughter was no different.

But while my wife and I had fallen in love at a young age, I would not let my daughter's heart be broken by a fool who didn't understand her or deserve her.

I can look back now, and see that my intentions were accurate and authentic, but at the time, they were vicious and barbaric.

To see tears in my little girl's eyes and know a boy put them there, that wasn't okay. It didn't matter how old she was or how mature she'd become.

There's one boy that paid the price for her breaking her heart that I will never forget.

This is the story you've been waiting for, Jack. The story that has never made the news and was never revealed during my trial...the story that my daughter finally discovered and came to see me about.

CHAPTER
EIGHT

POPS

Before I begin, Jack, I need to tell you something.

In the forty-plus years I have called this hell hole home, my daughter never came to visit.

Does that surprise you?

It shouldn't.

I specifically told her never to come. I wanted her to move on with her life, to not let what I'd done influence her in any way.

Sure, I know that's a hard ask because how could I not affect her...I am her father, the man who raised her, loved her, taught her everything she knows.

But I wanted...no, I needed to believe that she was okay, that she was doing well, and by coming to visit, whether it was on birthdays or during the holidays, she would be placing her life on hold to revisit the past.

I didn't want to be something she had to 'revisit'.

I never wanted to be something she had to deal with, overcome, tackle...if that makes any sense.

She came to visit a few weeks ago.

I should never have agreed to see her.

I wish I hadn't.

CHAPTER
NINE

POPS

I devised clever ways of getting rid of the boys who thought they were good enough for her throughout the years.

There's a reason they called me the Boyfriend Slayer.

I was charged with killing four men. The cops thought they had me, but it turns out they only found the bodies I didn't hide well enough.

In total, there were probably about seven, give or take, that I killed from the time Angel was fourteen to nineteen.

The first was found mauled by wolves in the woods.

The second, third and fourth, I fed to the pigs. Did you know pigs will eat just about anything? They can't digest hair or teeth, which took me about two bodies to figure out. Those things aren't hard to get rid of, though.

The fifth boy I chopped up and buried his body parts around our property. The cops found him and claimed him as my second victim. I didn't bother to correct them.

The sixth boy...well, I'll get to him soon enough.

The seventh boy I left in a public restroom off the interstate late one night. He and I met in a bar that was far from home, and I heard him boasting to his friends about my girl. Stupid prick should have shut up, especially after I made my presence known, but he didn't.

Guess he figured I wouldn't do anything to him since we'd been seen in public together.

He guessed wrong.

I didn't care that we'd been seen together. I didn't care that people heard me threatening to cut off his penis if he ever came near my girl again. I sure as hell didn't care when I clocked him good in the bar, and he was lights out while I finished my beer, paid my tab, and left.

I probably should have, because he's the one that got me caught. I wasn't too smart with him, even though it took the police a while to link us together.

I didn't plan to kill him, well...I didn't plan to kill him that night, that's for sure.

Two hours after I walked out of that bar, we met again. I'd pulled over to use the washroom on a side road and was just leaving when he opened the door and walked right into me.

It took me about three seconds to register who he was, and my fist connected with his face before he even took a step backward.

Let me paint the scene for you.

This side road was frequented by farm trucks hauling feed, and the only rest stop along that route. It was nowhere near where I lived, but then I was nowhere close to home either. I'd gone to take a look at a friend's truck, see if it was something I wanted to buy and fix, and he lived a solid hour away.

The rest stop had a two-stall washroom, with walls covered in graffiti, floors covered in grime and the one working sink wasn't fit for a horse to drink from.

By the time I was done with that boy, he was unrecognizable.

What did I do? I cut off both hands and feet after stuffing his mouth with his dick.

Yeah, I might have gone a little overkill on that one. But, he pissed me off.

Now, don't think I forgot about the sixth boy. I haven't. He's the story you're about to get. I thought I'd be taking him to the grave with me, but I was wrong.

He's why my daughter came to see me.

CHAPTER
TEN

POPS TO JACK

I don't regret any of the killings, Jack. I don't. I did what I needed to do in order to protect my daughter, to keep her safe.

I know they called me a serial killer, but I disagree with that title.

I've met actual serial killers, Jack. So have you. This place is full of them.

I'm not like them.

I'm not crazy.

I'm not driven by a need to kill.

I never kept a single trophy.

I killed those boys because I had no other choice.

Not all of their deaths were intentional. The first sure wasn't. I just wanted to teach him a lesson. It's his fault he didn't walk out of the woods fast enough, that he didn't stop his own bleeding, that he got caught by the wolves.

At this stage of my life, with Death waiting for me, I should have regrets, and I do; I have a lot of regrets, but not about killing anyone.

I regret not telling my wife I loved her more.

I regret not doing better as a husband.

I regret not being there to watch my daughter grow, to see her accomplishments with my own eyes.

I regret turning a blind eye when I could have helped someone here, in this place I call home.

There's a lot I regret, but that doesn't help me now, does it?

I specifically regret not doing more to make sure my daughter never knew about the sixth murder.

CHAPTER
ELEVEN

POPS

Everything changed when Angel turned eighteen. She'd finally graduated from high school, and she was ready for a life on her own.

Or so she thought. Most kids believe that, don't they?

My father died of a heart attack, and Angel wanted to stay with my mother, to help her. All my other sisters and brothers had their own families by this time, so I couldn't say no.

I wasn't happy about it, though. How could I protect her, ensure her safety if she wasn't beneath my roof?

I did what any father would do; I was a good son and visited my mother often. She was happy to have me around, and it was time for us to get to know one another, something that never happened while I had been a child.

I knew my siblings better than I had known my parents.

My daughter didn't appreciate me hovering over her. Not that I cared all that much. Children are finicky creatures, and they change their minds constantly.

She may be a woman in one sense, but in another, she was very naive.

I overheard her once confess to my mother that she was in

love. It was like my heart had been ripped out at the knowledge I would be left alone, yet again.

Being alone is the only thing I have ever feared. It's like a rope wrapped around my neck, a heavy burden that is always there.

I'm a strong man, I always have been, but this fear makes me weak, and I hate any sense of weakness in a man.

The man who claimed my daughter's heart was weak too.

A strong man would have made his claim clear. A strong man would have approached me, as her father, and asked for her hand in marriage. A strong man would have done everything to make sure my daughter was always protected.

He wasn't a strong man.

He stood by as his friends chased my daughter into a dark alley behind the grocery store. He watched as they kicked and punched and ripped her clothes off her. He stayed silent as they raped her, one by one by one, leaving her bloodied body there, in that back alley to be found by the grocer.

How is a father to remain sane when this happens to his child?

When I first saw her lying there in the hospital bed, I wanted revenge.

I wanted to hunt down the bastards that touched my daughter and tear them apart, destroy them, one by one, until it's all I could think, all I could see, all I wanted.

I would have gone after them, one by one, I would have killed them all but for my daughter.

She begged me to stay with her.

She begged me to wait with her.

She begged me to not leave her alone.

She had no one else. I had no one else. Of course, I stayed with her.

While she healed, she grew into a woman I often had glimmers of but never thought possible. As she recovered, she became a different woman. Not one who fought me, who wanted her freedom from me, but instead, she became a woman who sought my help, who wanted to learn from me.

From me - her father.

She wanted to learn how to get revenge, and I had no problem helping her with this.

Once she was released from the hospital, we returned to the farm where I raised her. We walked through the woods behind the house, setting traps, and hunted together. As she regained her strength, she would lose herself in work in the garage, rebuilding engines.

I was so proud of her.

We bonded and grew closer than we ever had.

After a while, there was a topic of conversation that kept coming back...revenge.

My baby girl needed revenge. Not just on the men who raped her but on the man who orchestrated it.

She made me promise that I wouldn't take this from her. I was her support, I had her back, but I also understood the need to avenge what had been done to her.

It tore me up, though, not to take care of it myself.

I watched those men. I knew where they worked, where they drank, where they lived. I shared all of this with my daughter and helped her to plan the next steps.

It was a Friday night.

Four drunken assholes walked out of a bar and had no idea they were being watched.

Three of them lived together.

Three of them died together.

They died in a house fire from a kicked over gas can and a discarded cigarette. My daughter might have kicked the can, making sure gas spilled all over the place, but it was the assholes themselves, flicking a cigarette over the back porch, that set the fire.

By the time the fire trucks arrived, it was too late.

Yes, we watched the house burn, waiting for the men to rush out of the house to escape the flames. No one did.

That left only one...the bastard she'd given her heart to.

CHAPTER
TWELVE

POPS TO JACK

You know, Jack, she didn't say a word as we sat there in the truck, watching the house burn.

She cried—a lot.

She gripped my hand. Hard.

But she never said a word.

I was so proud of her, am still so very proud of her.

Have you ever sought revenge?

Have you ever been hurt enough, so destroyed that the only way to heal was to enact revenge?

Most people have no concept of what revenge even means.

We all understand what being hurt means - what it's like to be betrayed by family or friends, to feel humiliated. We dream about placing those people in similar situations, so they understand what we went through.

When we act on those dreams, we think we've gotten our revenge.

Hell, most of the people on the floors below are here because of an act of revenge in one form or another. But we're the few, Jack.

Most people dream of revenge; they imagine what it would feel like, taste like, how it would empower them after losing their power...but it's rare anyone ever does anything about their revenge fantasies.

Think about it…how often do you dream about getting revenge and then do it? Actually, do it, Jack?

You not only think about what you would do, but you plan out the steps, you prepare yourself and the situation so that when the timing is right, you can act?

Well…okay, I'll give it to you that you may understand what I'm saying.

(This is Jack: I confessed some pretty fucked up things that I've done in the name of revenge to Pops. I'm not sure why other than I wanted him to know I understood what he was talking about. And no, I'm not going to share my confession with you. Pops is a dead man; who is he going to tell?)

As we watched that house burn, the effect was instantaneous for my daughter. I watched her transform, not wholly, not all the way, but it was a beginning, a start. The healing she needed, the knowledge that she was taking back her control, it came back the longer that house burned with no survivors inside.

She'd done what those assholes couldn't do. She survived the destruction.

But that healing wasn't complete. There was still one man who needed to be taught a lesson, and my daughter, was in the mood to be his teacher.

It was hard, Jack. Hard to not step in. Hard to not want to shelter her from what she was about to do.

But I didn't. Not then, at least.

CHAPTER
THIRTEEN

POPS

My daughter didn't act right away. She took her time, planned everything out just right.

I watched my daughter heal, and I have to tell you, it felt good to be there, to know I was a part of it.

After her rape, she became a breathing apparatus, barely living, barely being. You know what I mean? She lost her smile, lost her laughter, lost her appetite, and became unrecognizable.

Shortly after coming home, she'd shaved her head bald; it was a reminder of how the men would pull on it to keep her still, wrapping her long hair around their fists as a way to exert their power over her, and then later ejaculated all over it.

She'd said shaving it had been the first step in regaining her control.

I believed her.

After that fire, she let her hair regrow.

After that fire, she started to smile again.

After that fire, a sparkle reignited in her eyes.

Out on the farm, I'd created a shooting range, and she would spend hours back there, not just with her gun, but she picked up a bow and arrow and perfected her aim.

In the evenings, we would talk about possible scenarios on what she wanted to do to the asshole of an ex-boyfriend.

Should she shoot him in the head and end him right there and then, or did she want to prolong his misery?

She didn't want him to die too fast.

She wanted him to feel the pain of whatever it was she was going to do to him.

I suggested she shoot him with her arrows. A few in the legs. In the arms. Then aim for his heart.

She wanted to gut him, pull his intestines out and leave him there to rot, but not until after shooting him in both legs so he couldn't walk to help.

I saw a side of my daughter I never thought was there.

She could be brutal. Vindictive. Sadistic.

To be honest, I wasn't sure how I felt about this side of her. I had pangs of doubt, of worry. Once you step into the dark, it's hard to get out. It's possible...as long as you don't go too far.

I was afraid she'd gone too far to ever retreat.

With the fire... we'd assumed the drunken assholes would have escaped. The fire wasn't set with the intention for them to die. That was just a...bonus, you know?

I wanted to kill the ex-boyfriend. But I didn't want her to do it.

I wanted her to hurt him. Destroy him. Make him pay for what he did to her.

I didn't want his death on her head. There's no going back from that, from that intentional action.

She didn't agree with me.

So while she made a plan, I made my own too.

I never intended for her to find out about mine. That was a secret I have always intended to take with me to the grave if I could.

My only goal was that she believed I was on her side and that I'd do anything and everything to protect her. I wanted her to think I wouldn't steal her control away.

My sixth victim deserved everything that happened to him.

It was a Friday night. Mr. Big Shot got a promotion and was moving, which meant we had to speed up our timeline.

Here's what happens when you are faced with hiccups in a plan...you overreact, you make mistakes.

My daughter ended up making a few mistakes because she rushed.

There was a big send-off for the ex. He was well-liked in our town, created a name for himself, and he was one of the lucky ones who managed to get away - or so everyone thought.

He had no family left in town. No friends. Moving to the city was a big step, the right one for him, or everyone said.

He was so ready to leave everything behind that all he took with him were his personal things - a few boxes of clothes, books, and some personal things. It all fit in the back of his car. Mr. Hot Shot was given a new apartment that was fully furnished; imagine that.

On the night he left, my daughter and I waited for him just outside of town. See, the thing with our town, you had to take a few roads, make a few turns, before hitting the main highway.

We waited in a spot where there were no street lights, and with it being a Friday night, and late at that, not much traffic.

My daughter shot out the tires of his truck as he approached.

She also shot up the front end of his car, peppering his windshield with bullets.

His car swerved until it fell off the side of the road and into a deep enough creek. He was nose first in the water.

We waited for him to get out of the car and escape. We sat there, guns ready, but he never made it.

I convinced my daughter to leave. She'd come in her own car. I told her to head into town and sit herself down in a bar and stay there for a good long while.

I wanted her to be seen in public, just in case anything was said, or she was ever questioned.

As far as she was concerned, the asshole of an ex had died in that car, swallowed up by the creek water.

The bullets...they were the mistake my daughter made.

The plan was to haul his car from the creek and hide it in one of the many sheds I've got on my property. I'd bury the body beneath the shack, take apart the truck here and there and reuse the material as I saw fit.

No one would ever know.

She'd killed him. I helped to cover it up.

Everyone else would just assume Mr. Hot Shot was in the city and too big to come home for a visit.

I hooked up his car and took it home. It was dark enough out, late enough, that I didn't pass a soul either.

I parked that truck in the shed and took a good look at the body.

Imagine my surprise to find out the asshole wasn't dead. He was merely unconscious, still breathing, still very much alive.

I won't tell you how relieved I felt seeing his chest rise. It meant my daughter didn't kill him. She didn't have that stain on her soul.

Since he wasn't dead, though, I did what any father would do…I took the necessary steps to protect her.

I killed him myself. I had an old hunting rifle in the shed and shot him in the head, nice and quick.

The shed didn't have a wood floor. A hole in the floor had been dug awhile ago, and all I had to do was fill it back up once I dumped his body into it. I burned all his clothes and magazine he'd kept, in my fire pit, parked his car over his body, and drank a few too many beers by the fire.

I didn't see my daughter for a while after that. She moved back in with my mother and then did the one thing her mother always hoped she would do: she applied to college and got accepted.

My girl was thousands of miles away, living her life when I first got arrested.

That boy that I'd killed in that washroom…the cops finally figured out I'd been involved.

By then, I'd taken care of the car in the old shed. I stripped it down to it's metal frame, and any bullet holes the body had contained were gone. In fact, I sold most of it for scrap metal, and the shed itself had fallen down upon itself, with a bit of help from me.

By the time the cops came round the house, it was just one of many structures sprinkled throughout my fields that were run down. At the time of my conviction, no one had ever found that body, and no one was ever to find it either.

I'd hoped things to stay that way. Unfortunately, my daughter came to visit me otherwise.

CHAPTER
FOURTEEN

POPS TO JACK

After forty years, you wouldn't think having another body attributed to me would matter. Right?

My farm has passed a few hands by now, or so I'm told. The latest owner dug up the shed to expand one of his gardens or something, and guess what they found?

The local police contacted my daughter after doing an autopsy on the body and confirming the identity.

You're probably thinking my daughter came to visit to tell me about this, right?

You'd be wrong, Jack.

I'd already been told about the body. My lawyer had been in touch, so had the police.

I'd already told them my story of what went down.

But then my daughter had to show up.

When I first found out that she had arrived, I thought I would have a heart attack. Why would she be here? Now, after all this time?

I almost didn't want to see her…but it's been forty years. Something inside of me ached to see her face one last time.

Sure, we'd talked a few times. She called to tell me I was a grandpa, and I heard the little baby cry. She called when her husband had died and then she got married again. But that was it. There were a few Christmas cards here and there over the forty years, but I didn't want her to visit.

I told you that already, right?

At first, there were tears in both our eyes when I first saw her.

I thought it was tears of happiness, of sadness for what we'd missed, but I was wrong.

Those tears she shed, they were of anger.

I'd done the unthinkable to her, or so she believed. I handed her a life masked in lies and shame, apparently.

When the body had been dug up, they were able to confirm the cause of death—close shot to the head by a hunting rifle.

Specifically, my old Remington Model 760.

My daughter had used her handgun when she shot at the car, another one of the mistakes made in a rush, and knew right away that she hadn't been the one to kill her ex.

You would think she'd thank me for making sure the deed was done. No. She was pissed that I'd covered it up and never told her. She was pissed she hadn't taken the kill shot, and she was pissed I'd done it instead.

No matter what I'd done, no matter what I could have said...I wouldn't have won.

I asked her what she would have wanted me to do. The question seemed pointless. The man needed to die, and I was there.

In my opinion, she'd done what she needed to do to further her healing and take back the control she needed to feel. Right?

Again, wrong.

According to her, I should have told her.

I could have found her and brought her back so she could have taken the shot herself.

By taking the shot and covering it up, all I did was help her live a lie.

She thought she was a murderer—a killer.

She'd lived with that hanging over her head for forty years. I stole a life from her that she could have lived, if only she'd known she wasn't a killer.

I didn't and still don't see the big deal.

Apparently, it is, though.

She hates me. While she's never talked about me, never told my grandchildren about me, did everything she could to distance herself from me, she'd still loved me.

That changed.

I wasn't afraid of being here or even dying because I knew I wasn't alone. There has always been a connection between my daughter and me.

Until her visit.

She said she hated me. She said she would live the rest of her life without a thought or care for me in it. She said I might as well die now because, according to her, I was already dead.

When she left, I knew I'd never see her again.

Was it wrong of me to hope that one day, she'll see the big picture and realize that everything I've done was to protect her?

Even that last murder. It was all for her.

Something changed, though, inside me when she walked away.

That tether to her, it broke. Snapped apart. I never felt alone until then.

Even with all I've done, I had a daughter that I loved and loved me back all these years.

I still love her, but I'm dead to her.

I think that's why I'm dying, Jack. She willed it to be so and so I will be.

Every action I've taken in my life, since her birth, was to protect her. Every action was a sign of love - for her.

Even this one, I guess.

CHAPTER
FIFTEEN

JACK

There's twenty minutes left to my shift.

I've grabbed my Scotch and filled a glass and brought it to Pops, to sniff.

I should have done it earlier when he'd asked.

I've only been gone for fifteen minutes, give or take. Okay, maybe thirty, but he's already gone.

I raise the glass in a toast, wish Pops happiness wherever he may be, and down the shot in one.

It burns, but it's a good sort of burn.

I'm not sure how I feel about his story.

How are you supposed to react when someone admits to murder?

I've heard so many confessions by now, so many telling me the same thing - that they killed someone and had no regrets...it makes me wonder at the type of person I am when I have no emotional reaction to their confession.

Was he justified? Was his daughter justified? Is revenge ever fitting?

In the end, does it matter? The man is dead. His victims are gone. He's paid for his crime already, and in the end, the one thing he feared did come true.

Pops died alone, with no one by his side.

FARMER JOE

PATIENT 1001

CHAPTER
ONE

There are some cases that fascinate the media.

Farmer Joe is one of those cases.

I've heard of the man but never spoke to him before.

To be honest, the man disgusts me.

He's the type of man I'd prefer he met his end downstairs, rather than coming to my floor to breathe his last breath.

I've never been interested in his story, and I'm still not sure I am now, but one of the guards from his floor swears the man has a secret he's been dying to tell me. I guess he's been bragging about this secret for the past few years, to the point where one of the guards contacted the local authorities where Farmer Brown lived and had them reopen his case.

They didn't find any new victims, which isn't much of a surprise.

Farmer Joe may remind you of a particular 'other' farmer from Canada, the one that tried to save prostitutes only to feed them to his pigs. Remember that guy? Farmer Joe isn't him. This guy was before that Canadian psycho.

There have to be more farmers than you'd expect who get rid of their unmentionables to their farm animals. Pops was one of those men, and I'm sure there's more out there.

Makes you wonder if the pork you're eating is safe, doesn't it?

CHAPTER
TWO

I'm working on yearly reviews for my staff, one of my least favorite things to do in this job. If I can find something else to do...even if it's wiping someone's ass... I'll do it.

So when Jeff, one of the guards from the third floor, knocks on my door, I have no problem yelling, "come in."

"Hey Jack, have you talked to him yet?"

Him being Farmer Joe.

The same man who carries a stench that has to be seeped into his pores, a scent that makes me want to vomit every time I go near his room.

"Did you guys take away his shower privileges? Like, what the fuck, man." I push away from my desk and stretch my back. I've been sitting for way too long, and my ass cheeks hurt.

"You get used to it. He doesn't smell half as bad as he used to be. I was told when he first came here, he smelled like he'd bathed in shit."

"He still does," I say.

I swear that smell just won't leave him. The scent must be so deep in his skin that it's now part of his DNA.

"Have you talked to him?" Jeff asks me again. This isn't the first time since Farmer Joe joined us that Jeff has come up to check-in.

"You know, even if I do, I'm not going to share anything with you." Okay, that might be a lie. It depends on what he tells me.

Jeff gives me a one-finger salute. "He's got something big to share, I swear on my mother's grave."

Okay, now I know he's pushing too hard. "Your mother isn't even dead yet, you asshat. What's in it for you?" I know there has to be. A bet made downstairs, maybe. He's probably going to earn big coin if he can get the details from me.

"A solid hundred plus the Warden will invite me hunting."

I stroke the underside of my stubbly chin. "Hmm. Those are high stakes." Hunting with the Warden is a reward in and of itself, so I get why he's after me to talk to Joe.

"He doesn't have a story I want to hear."

Jeff gives me a shake of his head. "He does, trust me."

"What can he tell me that hasn't already been covered? The guy was all over the news, his farm basically bulldozed, and we know there are more victims out there than what was found. He killed prostitutes...so what?"

Don't get me wrong: I'm not saying that those lives aren't meaningful because of their profession. People are people, but adding one or two more of their deaths to the list isn't something I'm really wanting to hear. That's all.

"Did you know he had kids?" Jeff drops a bomb he knew would blow up at the right time.

"No..." I'm trying to think back over what I've read or heard about Farmer Joe. I don't ever recall him having kids. "How many?"

"Two boys."

"How did you find out?" My eyes narrow as I try to read the guard in front of me.

"Joe wanted to make sure he got time with you and knew he needed to give me something. I promised I'd try. Come on, man, this is huge. He had kids with him on that farm, kids no one knew about!" He's jumping from one foot to the other as he gets all worked up.

"What happened to the kids?"

"I don't know, man. That's what I'm telling you. You want to take his confession, I promise!"

I'll admit, there's a slight stirring of interest now with the question of his kids. Is this really new info or made up? Is it a last-ditch effort to tell me a story, and if so, why?

CHAPTER
THREE

I find Ike leaning against the hall, just outside Farmer Joe's room.

"He's getting a sponge bath," Ike wrinkles his nose. I copy him out of habit.

"Have you heard the rumors?" I ask.

"Jeff doesn't know how to keep his mouth shut." Ike's eye roll tells me he shares my same reservations about the farmer. "You talking about the fact he had kids?"

I nod. "I checked his file and even googled him. There's nothing about him having children or even a wife."

Ike nods. "Yeah, I did the same when Jeff first mentioned it. Think it's all true, though?"

I shrug. "Hell if I know. I haven't decided if I want to find out yet or not."

"That's a lot of time in the same room with him."

Trust me, I know.

"What if it is true? Could you imagine? What, did he feed his kids to the pigs too?"

It's a sick fuck who feeds humans to swine.

"You think I should hear his confession, don't you?"

Ike gives me a shrug of his shoulder. "It at least makes for an interesting story. Besides, we won't have to put up with his stench for long. I contacted poison control, and with the amount of poison he consumed, he won't last the night."

There's been issues of...leadership down on the third floor. Farmer Joe challenged the wrong inmate and paid the price with being forced to eat poisoned food. From what I hear, there's an internal inquiry into how the inmate in question had access to the poison, but that's none of my business.

It's not a good way to die, even for a farmer.

CHAPTER
FOUR

Other than the occasional scream or yell, the floor is relatively quiet.

As I drag my chair toward Farmer Joe's room, the wheels squeak and squeal as they have always done, incite a level of excitement among those still awake.

I hear the dull thuds of their fists hitting the sides of their beds, a steady drum as I make my way to listen to a confession I wasn't sure I wanted to take.

Farmer Joe isn't a handsome man. He's got a thick, broad forehead, bald head, a gut that resembles a beach volleyball beneath the blankets.

He still smells.

I notice one of the far windows has been opened slightly, which is never allowed unless the patients are strapped to the bed.

In this case, even if Farmer Joe wasn't in straps, I'd need that window opened.

Thankfully, his ankles are wrapped in restraints, a necessary precaution. Even with the poison eating his insides away, he could still find an ounce of supernatural strength at the end and hurt someone.

I've seen it happen more times than I want to count, all

because someone on my staff didn't take the necessary precautions.

Farmer Joe is looking at me, and there's a wildness in his gaze that I wasn't expecting.

"The Angel of Death has come, has he? I've been waiting a long time for you. I wasn't sure if you were real or an imagined nightmare."

"I'm very real, Joe, and yes, I've come for you."

Eating human-fed pig meat can harm a person in many ways. Prion diseases can be manifested with symptoms of hallucinations, dementia, difficulty walking with muscle soreness, and confusion, among the few.

Farmer Joe has been on medications for years since coming here to us. Medicines that have slowed the disease, but there's only so much medicine can do after years of eating tainted meat.

I've sat at the bedside of many who were delusional, lived with hallucinations, and such. I have their confessions, for what they were. Often, they were simply senseless stories.

I have no doubt that's what this one will be, as well.

"Are you friendly, Death? I've heard if I tell you a good story, you'll walk me through the pearly gates. Is that true?"

I can't help but laugh at that. Is that what they're saying about me on the lower floors?

"If there are pearly gates, that's up to fate to decide whether you walk through them. I'll listen to your story but on one condition." I lean forward, as close as a I dare, and stare Farmer Joe straight in the eyes. "The story you tell me, it must be one you've never told. Do you understand?"

His head bobs, his double chin merging into the skin of his chest.

"Stories are journeys, don't you think Death Angel? I've been on a journey that only the dead have shared with me. No one alive has heard this story, I made sure of it." His voice is hoarse, scratchy, and I can only imagine how rough his throat must feel.

I'm surprised he's even able to talk, to tell the truth. I know the poison is eating the stomach lining and more, but I can only imagine the damage to his throat as it was swallowed.

He coughs, but he's on enough medication that he doesn't feel the pain despite the spittle of blood that now coats his mouth.

"Maybe you should save your story for when you're at the gates?" I suggest. "You can tell it to me then."

He shakes his head. "You won't be joining me on that journey, will you? I tell you now, while I can. I may be a crazy man, but I'm not a dumb one."

CHAPTER
FIVE

FARMER JOE TO JACK

I'm a man who never should have been a father.

Yes, you heard me right.

Let's face it, I'm probably a man that shouldn't have been born. Both my mother and father told me that from an early age. I've always believed them.

I count every year I'm alive as a gift. Well, I did until I came here.

I wish I had died with my pigs rather than come here. I should have killed myself before I'd been caught. I'd tried to...but I guess for a man who shouldn't have been born, it's pretty hard to kill him.

Hell, I'm supposed to be dead already, don't you think? Hopefully, I'll stay alive long enough to share my secret. Everyone else who knows about it is gone.

I'm a simple man. Always have been. Give me food from my farm to eat, something soft to sleep on, and clothes to keep me warm. I don't need much, never have. Never cared about being rich or being 'somebody' in life.

I'm a simple farmer. My father was a simple farmer, and his father before him.

I know there's been a lot of stories about me, most of them aren't true.

Most of what I said to my lawyer or to the cops got twisted, and that ain't, sorry, wasn't right.

I may be simple, but I don't have to talk like a simpleton - that's what my guard downstairs says all the time. He would read things to me, you know? And correct me with how I say things. He says my speech was part of the problem, why I was painted in such a disgusting light.

Why can't people just see you for who you are without trying to see something that ain't, sorry, isn't there.

I've been painted a monster. I'm not one, whether you believe me or not.

CHAPTER
SIX

FARMER JOE

My parents died when I was just a teen.

First, my Momma. Daddy always told me she had a heart attack out in her vegetable garden and that by the time he got to her, the pigs had found her first.

We had two pet pigs who roamed the farm, free to eat whatever they wanted. They were also our house pets, sleeping first in my bed when they were just tiny piglets, then on the floor when they became too big.

The other pigs, they weren't pets. They were livestock to be fed, fatted, and then later sold.

I'm not sure who got to Momma first...it might have been Bertha or George. By the time Daddy got there, they were both... enjoying her.

Pigs eat anything, you know? Well...not everything, but they'll try. They love skin, muscle, and fat. They love to break bones and tear limbs. All they want to do is eat. Eat and eat and eat some more.

Daddy said that by eating Momma, they were special. We could never kill them now, but we had to honor their death when the time came, as they honored Momma.

So we never killed them. We let them live until they died on their own. And then we ate them.

Sometimes, at night, I'd hear Daddy talking to George and Bertha down by the fire. He talked to them as if Momma was part of them, as if she could hear him.

So did I.

She could, you know. She heard us. I always felt better after talking to them. After Momma died, whenever I was sad or crying because Daddy whipped me over good, Bertha would come over and place her snout on my shoulder. She never did that before.

That was Momma comforting me. I believe it.

It was always just Daddy and me on the farm. Sometimes he'd have some foreigners come and help during the spring and summer, and they'd sleep in one of the cabins Daddy had built just for them. They even had a section of the garden to grow their own food, and sometimes they brought their whole family with them, their women would cook and garden, kids would help with the pigs and play with me, sometimes.

Schooling wasn't that important to Daddy. I'd go when I could, but I only got to grade seven before he said he needed me on the farm more than the teacher needed me filling a desk. The real work, the only work I needed to be prepared for, was at the farm.

He was a hard man, my Daddy. He lived a hard life and the hand he raised me with was just as hard.

He didn't believe in God either. Raised me to believe there's nothing after this life, that the only thing our bodies are good for is nutrients for the ground or for the animals, like what happened to my mom.

Me, I like to think there's something after this, you know? Those pearly gates the preacher downstairs talks about all the time. I'd be okay if someone was there to greet me, saying that I did the best with what I had.

I only want to be judged on that merit, you know?

Daddy, I think he always knew he was going to die early, you know?

I just turned nineteen, became a real man, when he took me

into the bank and signed everything over to me. The farm, it was in the clear with no payments left on it other than the credit Daddy took out to help with bills. That was easy enough to pay; a few pigs a month to the local butcher always took care of that, he told me.

I didn't take any debt when it was just me. The pigs and I, we did just fine.

About six months after everything ended up being in my name, I woke up one morning to a note on the table. I knew Daddy was sick. His body had deteriorated over the past few months, and his legs could barely hold him up anymore. He told me the end was here, and he wanted to go the only way he knew. His note told me to bury whatever was left of him beside Momma's grave, beneath a large copse of trees in the back end of the property.

A part of me always wished he'd said goodbye, you know?

Looking back, the night before had probably been one of the best in my life. Daddy and I hung out together all day. I'd take care of the pigs, and then he sat at the table while I made us something to eat. He'd asked me to make a dish my Momma always made when I was little. It didn't taste the same, but he said nothing about it. We spent the night in front of the television and even shared a few beers.

By the time I was ready for bed, Daddy had fallen asleep in his chair, so I covered him up with his blanket, put a few more logs in the fireplace, and went to bed.

I wish I'd known that was the last I'd see him.

I would have told him...that I loved him, I guess. That was a word we never used, and I don't ever remember hearing it from him, but I would have said it.

I would have.

He wasn't in the chair when I woke up.

He wasn't out in the barn or in the field, either.

I found his shirt and pants hanging off the fence posts where we keep the family pigs.

That's when I knew what he'd done.

It hurt, but that was the way of us men in this family. We lived by the pig, and we died by them too.

I didn't know any different then. I do now.

I wish I were back on my farm. I wish I could see my pigs again. I wish I could feel the heat of their snouts on my skin as I die.

CHAPTER
SEVEN

FARMER JOE TO JACK

You don't know of any farmers nearby, do you, Death Angel? Any with pigs? Any looking for a free meal?

You're looking a little green around the gills. Does the idea of how I want to die bother you? Why?

I hate knowing I'm dying in this place. I only ever wanted to die at home, on my farm, in peace, you know?

How about you? Have you thought about how you want to die? Probably not in one of these beds, right?

Downstairs, we'd often talk about that - death and how we want to meet our end. Some men want to die while having sex. Others want to go in their sleep. Some want to die in the same way they made their kills.

Me...feed me to nature. I sure as hell don't want to be cremated - do you hear me? Do not put my body in that incinerator you've got in the basement. I'll haunt you for the rest of my life if you do that.

Hack me up into pieces if you need to. Put me in a garbage bag and drop me in a pig trough. I'll be a happy man.

Oh, sorry, shouldn't I have said that? Come on, Death Angel, you've heard worse, I'm sure. You know of the Director, right? The Funeral

Director? The one who used to feed the dead to their families? Come on…how can what I want be any worse?

Listen, do me a favor, will you? When the Director comes up here, ask him if he has a special recipe he'd use for you.

No? You don't want to do that? Well, you're not much fun, are you?

What's that? Don't threaten me with leaving, don't be like that. Fine, I'll get back to my story.

What did you think of my Daddy? I hope I didn't paint him in a bad light. He was a hard man who lived a hard life, and he raised me to be strong for when life got difficult.

I miss him.

I was all alone then after he died. A man goes stir crazy, you know, in the dead of night, when left alone.

Sometimes I'd go into town, to one of the bars, and I'd find a woman to keep me company. I had to clean up real good before I went; otherwise, the women turned up their noses at me.

I'm a pig farmer. Of course, I smell. But a dollar is a dollar, right?

There was one woman I…well, I think I fell in love with her.

No one knew about her, not till now. Now you'll be the only one I tell.

CHAPTER
EIGHT

FARMER JOE

I met her in a parking lot one night when I was leaving the bar.

She told me her name was Lily. She was beautiful. She had the softest skin, hair that was almost white, like her name, and her voice was like a song.

I'd never seen a creature like her before. Never met one, face to face.

I stammered like a simpleton, but she made me feel so comfortable. I didn't need to say much to her, but it was like she knew what I couldn't say.

We were two lonely souls that met for one memorable moment, and I...well, I was addicted.

Lily was all I could think about. I'd rush through the chores just to drive into town and wait for her. We never met in public, where people would see us. It was always in private. I'm not sure why, but it just worked out that way.

In the end, it was for the best.

She remained my own little secret, something no one knew about.

It surprised me no one ever found out about her, especially

when my whole life was plastered for everyone to see and judge. I waited, you know? Waited for someone to come across something and out her, us, but no one ever did.

You're the only one to know about Lily. It's nice being able to talk about her, finally.

Lily was special. She didn't mind who I was or what I did. She didn't mind the smell either.

At first, we would meet once a week. I'd go into the bar, have my drink or two, then wait out in my truck. It didn't matter how long I had to wait; I'd wait for hours if needed.

We never stayed there, in that parking lot. We would go for drives, leave town and head down the back roads. Sometimes we'd stop in farmer fields for midnight picnics. Other times, we'd make love in the truck.

At first, I paid. Then, she stopped seeking payments and told me to save the money to buy her a nice ring instead.

Lily loved me as much as I loved her. She came from a simple life too, and understood what a hard day's work meant.

We had so much in common, too. We were only children, and both our parents were gone. While I lived in a farmhouse all by myself, she rented a room from someone in town and had nothing to call her own.

Until we found out she was pregnant with my child.

I know what you're thinking: how can I be sure it was my child, right?

We just knew. I was the only man she was sleeping with by then. She still worked the streets, but she stopped having sex. She promised me she did, and so I believed her.

I loved her. Of course, I believed her.

The minute she told me she was pregnant, everything changed for me then.

Having a baby meant we wouldn't be alone anymore.

I told her to come and live with me, out on the farm.

By then, it was only me. I stopped letting the foreigners come and stay, I didn't really need them, and I know Daddy did it to be nice and so I'd have kids to play with. Well, I wasn't a kid anymore, and I didn't have to be nice. Besides, I was able to manage the livestock I had. Pigs, they take a lot of work, but it's muscle memory work, you know? I had chickens and a few cows too. Enough, but not too many.

When she moved in with me, Lily helped with the cows and chickens, plus she took over Mommy's garden. She was so excited to get in that soil and plant things. She said her dream was always to live on a farm with animals, and I was her dream come true.

She was my dream come true too.

I never knew what to expect when it came to women having babies. Sure, I knew what it was like with the animals, but women, they're different creatures.

Lily didn't like being pregnant. She was sick every day and had horrible pains. She wouldn't go to the doctor because the doctors killed her parents, so we made do as best we could. I made sure she didn't do too much. The farther along she got she eventually just stayed in bed. I finally moved the bed into the living room so she could watch television during the day while I was in the barn, working.

We used to talk, late at night, about the baby. We had grand dreams, the two of us. We wanted to have a large family, and she wanted to have a little girl. Me, I wanted a boy, someone who could take over the farm for me.

We wanted our babies to go to school. That was important to both of us. Our children, they had to be better than us. We wanted them to do better with their lives than be pig farmers. We dreamed of having a doctor and a lawyer, a teacher, and a restaurant owner. We wanted our kids to have the world and everything that came with it.

Lily and I…we were happy people. We were simple people but happy people. We lived in a dream world, a world where anything and everything could happen, if only we believed in it hard enough.

We were stupid and naive.

When Lily's water broke, everything changed.

All our dreams were destroyed within a matter of hours, and that perfect life we thought we had, was gone.

It was gone, and in its place, was a nightmare.

CHAPTER
NINE

FARMER JOE TO JACK

I supposed Death Angels can't be fathers, can they?

You know, until I was one, I didn't want to be a father. I didn't think I had it in me. When I became a Daddy, it changed me.

Being a parent is the most challenging job out there.

My whole life changed in an instant. When people tell you that - they don't lie.

(Jack here: Farmer Joe pauses here for a few minutes. I'm not sure if he's finding it difficult to talk or if it's the subject he's finding difficult. His heart rate is a little low, and even with the oxygen, he's having a hard time breathing. I'm suggesting we stop, but he shakes his head.)

I told you I had a secret. So, here it is: My Lily gave birth to twins.

Can you imagine that? Two boys.

But then the unthinkable happened.

She died giving birth. The boys, they tore her apart, literally, as they were born.

I remember the first time I saw them, the first head as it crowned, then the shoulders and a portion of the back, and then…he was stuck. No matter how hard she pushed, he wouldn't budge.

I've helped plenty of my animals give birth. I've been there during the difficult ones and the easy ones. This…this was different.

I had to help. As I would with a cow or the pig, I had to get in there and do what needed to be done. Except, it didn't matter how much I tried to help get that baby out of her, it tore her in two, and the blood just wouldn't stop…no matter what I did.

I figured I was going to lose them both.

Then I realized something. There were two babies.

By now, my Lily, she was gone. First, she'd lost consciousness, then with the blood that wouldn't stop, she just lost her life.

But the babies, I could save the babies.

So I did what needed to be done. I cut her open and pulled out those boys.

They were beautiful. They were precious.

They were also monsters, and I had no idea just how much my life just changed.

CHAPTER TEN

FARMER JOE

Conjoined twins. That's what my boys were. They were joined at the hips, or pelvis, bum to bum.

If it weren't for that, they were perfect. Both had two sets of arms, two sets of legs, two penises. They shared hips and a bum.

I honestly didn't think they would survive. How could they, like that?

I didn't know what to do.

I should have taken them to the hospital; that's what I should have done. But, my instincts kicked in, and I thought about what I'd do if this were one of my animals born with some deformity.

Most of the time, I'd put them out of their misery right away.

Other times I'd let nature lead me. I've had three-legged pigs. I've had animals with bum feet. They find ways to survive.

The life I live, the life I see lived daily, as a farmer, is the fight to survive. The strongest win. The weak die.

Lily, she was dead. There wasn't much I could do about that.

I cleaned her up, said my goodbye, and did what I'd been taught to do.

I fed her to the pigs.

Now the boys, I wasn't sure what to do with them.

My instincts kicked in, I guess, and I did what I could to keep them comfortable for as long as they were with me.

I had a warming pen that I made into their crib. They slept on their sides, and I turned them every few hours. Lily had made some cloth diapers that obviously weren't going to work, so I cut them and figured out a way to wrap them around the boys.

I figured their stomachs worked just fine considering the amount of shit that came out of that single ass of theirs. I bottle-fed them, kept them warm and clean, and waited for them to die.

Except, they never did.

I made a type of sling/swing contraption that would hold them upright, so they weren't always lying on their sides. They seemed to like that.

I wasn't sure if they were aware of each other, but I guess being attached to someone like they were would be hard not to be aware there was something always at your back. They would touch each other, hold hands, bang heads together, find ways to soothe the other when they cried.

It was interesting to watch.

I honestly thought they weren't going to survive long. But other than the obvious, they were perfectly healthy.

Those first few years, man, they were hard.

I had to figure how to dress them, becoming creative with a sewing needle.

Teaching them how to walk…that was…well, I guess you could say it was interesting. The boys learned the side step, and I fashioned a scooter type set up that they could move around the floor easier. Once they figured out how to use it, it was hard to keep them in one area. As they grew, so did the scooter to fit their needs.

I never did take them to a doctor. They never saw another person either. I kept them hidden whenever anyone arrived and any errands I had to run, I did it while they were asleep.

Life was good, you know? Other than raising two boys, it was fine. I wasn't alone anymore, and once we passed their second year, I got used to the idea that I wouldn't be alone ever again. Don't get me wrong, life wasn't easy, not by a long shot.

I missed Lily. I missed having another adult to talk to. I missed what it meant to have her in my life. If she'd lived, life would have been a little bit easier, I'm sure.

David and Michael, that's what I ended up calling them. I don't mind giving you their names. Since they're not alive anymore, it doesn't matter that you know.

They were named after my father and grandfather, and they were the name Lily had decided on if we were to have a son.

I don't remember what we'd picked for a girl. Flower names, like hers, I think. Not that it matters anymore.

Now that I think about it, most of the names I gave any of the animals, I named them after flowers. We had Rose, Violet, Petunia, Daffodil, to name a few. I never had a Lily, though. There has only ever been one Lily in my life, and no one could ever replace her.

Raising boys as a single father, much less twin boys joined like they were, fuck, it wasn't easy. I don't know what it would have been like with one son, or twins that were normal, but joined like they were, it brought about a whole new set of problems. Like how they went to the bathroom and cleaned themselves. Like how we dealt with puberty and giving each other some privacy.

Oh good heavens, personal space, that wasn't a thing, not between the two, but it didn't mean they didn't need it.

Puberty was…interesting.

Living on the farm, procreation was an everyday thing.

Sex…between animals, sure.

Between humans…how was I supposed to teach them that?

The likelihood they would ever see another female, much less have sex with one, wasn't something I'd thought about.

I think I always knew that because the boys were different, life would be different for them. I never expected them to live to adulthood, and the fact they had as many birthdays as they did was nothing short of a miracle.

The boys themselves were so different.

Everything seemed to be easy for Michael. He figured out how to walk, how to talk, how to maneuver to get what he wanted faster than David. He was the dominant one.

David…he had the temper. Nothing came easy. Everything was difficult. His legs were weaker than Michael's; he got sick more often too. I constantly worried that he would die while Michael lived…I knew what would have to happen, but I prayed I'd never be forced to kill my own child.

I wasn't that kind of monster.

CHAPTER
ELEVEN

FARMER JOE TO JACK

I know what the news said about me.

I know how I was demonized, called a monster, and worse.

I saw those interviews, read those articles, heard all the evidence they found to convict me.

(Jack here: Farmer Joe stops as I put some ice chips on his lips. His breathing is ragged, and there's a flare of red on his face. He was getting a bit heated and needs a bit of a break.)

Do you have any idea what it's like to be condemned like I was? I'm a simple man but not a simpleton. I understand right from wrong. I respect nature, understand the cycle of life.

I may be a pig farmer, but I'm still human.

I was made to sound like an animal, with only animalistic instincts, and that wasn't fair.

I wasn't any of the things they said I was.

I'm not an evil man - my Daddy didn't raise me to be.

I didn't kill all the women they said I killed.

Does that surprise you, Death Angel?

Talking is starting to hurt now. Think you could give me another shot for the pain?

Thank you.

Have you put the pieces together yet?

Have I painted enough of a picture for you to understand what might have happened?

No? Well, let me tell you then…

CHAPTER
TWELVE

FARMER JOE

By the time the boys were sixteen, I knew they didn't have much longer to live. A few years, maybe. Michael, he could have lived into his twenties, I'm sure of it.

David...not him.

Even at that age, you could see how weak he was. The boy couldn't be on his feet long before the muscles would give out. Sometimes walking across the room, even with Michael doing most of the work, the boy would be out of breath, complaining his chest hurt too much.

That wasn't the only thing different about the two boys. One rarely got upset about anything, the other...he was always upset, about everything too.

David's explosive anger dictated a lot of our life. I'm not much of an angry man, never have been. Daddy said I had a long fuse, like him. David's, though, it was shorter than my pinkie finger. Didn't take much to set him off.

Looking back, well... I'd talk to Doc downstairs, you know, on my floor? His room was four down from mine, and he's a crazy bugger, that's for sure. But we've had our talks over the years. I would make it sound like Daddy had a short fuse just so I could understand where it came from. I don't think Daddy minds that I've lied about him over the years, do you? I'm hoping I'll have a chance to ask him, that he'll be there too when I die.

Doc says the short fuse isn't so much from anger but frustration. It kind of makes sense, the more I think about it. The boy couldn't do much. His legs were weak, his heart was weak, he was always less than his brother, at least, in his own eyes.

Michael, now he was a good boy. He did what he could to keep the peace, to help his brother out, but there was only so much either one of us could do, you know what I mean?

Do you remember what it was like when you were sixteen?

I do.

Even before that age, Daddy gave me some of his magazines around to help me out. It's like our brains are all over the place, all we focus on is what makes us feel good and sex…that sure makes us feel good, doesn't it?

I thought maybe it would help the boys, you know?

A few times, when I was alone and watching one of my porno videos, I'd catch the boys at their bedroom door, watching too. I never said anything about it, just went about my business while they went about theirs.

I never brought a woman home, not after the boys were born. I didn't want anyone to see them, to know about them, you know?

Almost every time I went into town for errands, I'd give in to my guilty pleasure. I didn't go into the bars, but the women, you could always find them. We'd do it in my truck, or I'd rent a room by the half-hour at the motel just on the outskirts of town.

I started to think about the boys, though, wondering how they'd like to experience a woman for once. I knew Michael would have no problem, but David had a hard time getting it up, you know? I thought maybe watching the porn wasn't enough for him; maybe he needed to feel it happening too and not just by his own hand.

I don't know. Saying it out loud, I know I was desperate. I

wanted the boys to live a full life, you know? Or as full as I could give them.

I didn't know if they could have sex like normal men, but that didn't mean they couldn't try, right? Or at least, get a good blow job.

I talked to the boys about it once.

I asked them if they wanted to have sex with a woman.

David laughed and said that would never happen.

Michael though, well, he had this look in his eye. I knew he wanted it. He asked how it would happen. I told him to think about some of the positions in the video, that it wouldn't be that difficult to figure out.

One day, the boys wanted to have a talk with me. Guess they'd talked about things, and they wanted to see if they could have sex with a woman. Michael suggested they could take turns, one at a time, with the woman on the edge of the mattress, if we brought it down to the floor. This way, the boys could each be on their knees, and there wouldn't be too much pressure for David with standing.

I was proud of them for figuring it out, you know?

It didn't happen right away; I took my time finding the right woman.

The first one was Gracie. I wanted to make sure I brought home a girl who knew what she was doing, you know? Who wouldn't get scared by what she saw or was going to happen.

I told her I'd pay extra. I figured I'd have to pretty the pot once we got to the house and she saw what was about to happen, but I'd deal with that when we got there.

Gracie was a sweetie. She knew it would be their first time.

I didn't tell her much about them, just that they had some health issues and a disability. I did mention that they couldn't have sex the usual way, but she just laughed and said that wouldn't be a problem.

I'll give her credit - she didn't run out the door when she saw the boys. She suggested a round of beers for everyone before she started to undress.

Did I stick around and watch? No. I left once they were ready to be alone, but you can bet I stayed close to the door, just in case, you know?

We moved the mattress to the floor, and I remember the sweet smile on her face when she told me I could leave. She said she'd take care of the boys good and proper and not to worry.

I wasn't worried...much.

CHAPTER
THIRTEEN

FARMER JOE TO JACK

So, bet you are judging me, aren't you?

Thinking I'm a horrible father?

You'd be right.

What kind of father brings a hooker into their home so his kids can get laid?

Well…one who knows their kids won't last long, that's who.

That's another thing I realized after chatting with Doc. Well, not just Doc, but the real shrinks they've got in this place.

No, I told them nothing about the boys, but once you've had to sit in therapy sessions for a long time…both in group and individual, you start to realize things on your own, you know?

(Jack here: Joe's eyes just closed, and he's stopped talking. Let's hope it's just for a breather.)

You ever sat in those group sessions, Death Angel? You should. You'd hear all sorts of things that would shock you. There's some nasty folks here, you know?

Yeah, I'm sure you do. You see enough of us, especially at the end, don't you?

At the time, I thought I was doing the right thing.

I didn't have anyone telling me different. No parenting books. No parents of my own to ask. I went by my gut and what I remember from Daddy. That's how I raised those boys, and I have no regrets.

None.

Don't look at me like that. You weren't there. You didn't live with us. If I'd taken those boys to the hospital, they would have asked about Lily. I couldn't have anyone knowing about her. They would have taken them boys from me, too. Don't try to tell me otherwise.

I may not have known how to be a parent, but they didn't know that.

As far as those boys were concerned, I was the best damn thing in their world. I cleaned them. I fed them. I loved them as best I could. I made it so that they didn't have to lie in a bed, being turned over on their sides every twelve hours or so, for the rest of their lives.

I may not know much, certainly less then than now, but I did the best I could to make sure they had a good life.

That's what being a parent is all about.

When it comes to that, I have no regrets.

Well…I guess I do have regrets.

Things would have turned out differently for me if I'd never brought Gracie home. The boys would have died a natural death. I would have fed them to the pigs, like their mother and my parents before them. No one would have known.

I would never have gotten caught. Never.

What's that? Yeah, I'm sure.

How would anyone have found out? The pigs? No, not from the pigs.

I never sold any of the pigs that ate my family. I kept them for myself. Despite what was on the news, the pigs that were sold to the local butchers and such, were all fine.

I swear on the good Lord above that I'm telling you the truth. That should get me past those pearly gates, right?

CHAPTER
FOURTEEN

FARMER JOE

Sorry if this next part gets uncomfortable. I'll admit that I made many mistakes and probably did everything the parenting handbooks say not to do.

While Gracie was busy with the boys in the bedroom, I took care of myself out in the living room. I kept an ear out, just in case, you know, but I probably dozed off a minute or two, if I'm being honest.

There was a bunch of noise coming from the room, but I hesitated going to the door, I mean…it was awkward enough that I'd brought a prostitute home for the boys, they didn't need their Daddy checking in to make sure things were going okay.

I probably should have.

No, I definitely should have.

First, Michael started yelling. Then David began screaming. I rushed to the door, threw it open, and I'll never forget the looks on the boys' faces.

David was pure ecstatic emotion. His face was red, his eyes lit up like sparklers, and the way his mouth was stretched...I couldn't be sure if it was a scream or a laugh.

Michael, that boy wore the face of pure fear. Tears slide down his face, hands fisted against his chest as he just looked at me, needing me to come in and save them both.

Gracie...well, Gracie was dead. I knew right away.

"What happened, boys?" There was so much that I wanted to say, but I knew I needed to remain calm. If I was calm, the boys would follow suit, or at least, that's what I hoped would happen.

Michael said nothing. David looked at Gracie, then me, then back to the woman.

"She laughed at me." That's all he said, and that's all he needed to say.

If there's one thing that boy of mine doesn't like, it's being laughed at.

"She was trying to help you." Michael's head was bowed, but I heard him clear as day. "She wasn't laughing at you, she was trying to help you."

"She laughed." David twisted his head, his lips puckered up tight. "She laughed and said...she said..." David started sputtering his words, he was wound up so tight.

"She said it's okay," Michael said, now crying in earnest. "She said it was okay, and you killed her for it."

David had no reply. He stared at Gracie, his hands going around his penis. "See, I can get it up. She didn't have to laugh."

He stared down at his growing dick, and yeah, it was pretty clear my boy didn't have an issue.

I don't know how long we stayed like that. It was a bit, though.

"Well," I cleared my throat, not sure what to say yet. "I think you boys need to clean up, get some pants on, while I take care of Gracie here. It's a shame, it is. I liked her."

I picked up Gracie in my arms, cradled her as nice I could. Who would have thought David had the strength to strangle her like he did, but sure enough, the bruises were there.

The boys remained where they were until after I left the room.

I did the only thing I knew to do. I carried Gracie out to the barn, selected the pen of our pet pigs, and laid her in the hay. She'd pissed herself at one point, and I knew the buggers would smell it.

I can still hear their snorts.

By the time I made it back into the house, the boys were in the kitchen.

"What are we going to do?" Michael asks.

"Nothing," David answered for me. "We're doing nothing, right?"

I nod in reply. That's exactly what we were going to do. Absolutely nothing.

I made sure there was no trace of Gracie in my truck, tossed her purse and things into the fire pit outside, and that night, we sat there and watched it burn.

It was a good month before I made my way back into town. I was nervous at first. I figured everyone would know by then that the pig farmer had taken a prostitute home. Every time I caught someone's gaze at the grocery store or the gas station, I figured they'd call the local police to let them know where I was.

Nothing happened. I made it home without anyone stopping me.

Gracie wasn't the first woman I brought home for the boys over the next two years. David quickly figured out that the only way for him to get hard and stay that way was by violence. I found some videos that he liked, and he'd watch them over and over. But watching and doing are two different things.

Each time he asked me to bring someone home, he promised he would be good. He swore he'd only hurt them a little, and I always believed him.

I shouldn't have.

I started having to drive to further places to find women to bring home. I made sure they were all older women, women with plenty of experience, who could help David figure out how far to go and when to stop. I always made sure I picked them up in dark places where no one else was around.

In the course of the next few years, I probably brought a woman home every four months. They all died in the end.

Michael didn't always have a go at the women. He usually went first, but sometimes he'd just let David have his fun.

I didn't realize it till later that David liked to keep things from each woman. Mainly, their underwear. I didn't think anything of it, why would I? I have a few pairs I've kept over the years as well. They keep you company in the middle of the night, you know?

Looking back, I should have tossed all those lacy things into the fire. If I had…I might not be in here.

That's how I got caught, you know?

After the boys died, I brought home someone to stay for a bit. Rachel, that was her name. I never killed her. Never hurt her. I treated her well and even showered every day for her. She found the box where I kept all the underwear and stole some. After a while, she wanted to leave, and so I took her back into town.

It wasn't long after that the police showed up.

I guess word had gotten out that women were going missing, and the hookers, well, they all decided to team up and keep each other safe. That woman, Rachel, gave the police the underwear and told them where I lived.

The rest is history, as you could say. They arrested me, tore my farm apart, did some tests on the pigs, found some bone fragments and whatnot, and here I am.

Do you remember when that other pig farmer, the one from Canada, hit the news? I wonder if he stole his ideas from me, eh?

CHAPTER
FIFTEEN

FARMER JOE TO JACK

What happened to the boys?

Well, they died just like I said they would.

David got sick with a cold one winter and never quite recovered. He went to sleep one night and just never woke up.

What was Michael supposed to do then? I'm not sure many organs the boys shared or didn't share, but they were attached. When David died, of course, it affected Michael. You gotta think they shared the same blood right?

(Farmer Joe stopped talking for a bit. I checked his pulse, it was weak but still there. I don't think Joe has much time left, to be honest)

I found both the boys dead in the morning. I figured David went first. I think we all knew what was going to happen. I told them I loved them the night before. I'd never said that before, not to them. They knew, of course, they knew, but I wasn't raised with words of love or praise, and so, I didn't raise the boys like that.

I showed love with my actions.

It was rough that morning, saying goodbye to the boys. I got more years with them than I'd expected. God was kind to me in that way.

Just like my Mommy and Daddy were fed to the pigs, so too were my boys. That's what we did; that's how we said goodbye.

I'm hoping they'll all be there, at the pearly gates, waiting for me. Do you think they will .....

(Jack here...Farmer Joe closed his eyes. I thought he was taking another break, but instead, he stopped breathing altogether. I'm not sure if his boys are waiting for him...I try hard not to judge my patients, but after this confession, I'm not sure he deserves to be seeing any pearly gates, do you?)

CHAPTER
SIXTEEN

JACK

Some confessions wear on me. Others don't affect me at all.

This one... I'm not sure how I feel at the moment.

It doesn't really matter if I believe him or not. He spoke with conviction, and I'm sure, to him, he was expressing his truth.

One person's truth and the real truth are often two different things, have you ever noticed that? For some, their ability to lie is so commonplace that they fall into their own trap of believing the lie.

Did Farmer Joe have children? It's possible.

The likelihood they were twins and conjoined... I'm struggling with that. There are so many medical complications that arise with conjoined siblings that I'm finding it hard to believe he never took them to the hospital, never got help, and that they lived until they were almost fifteen.

I'm not saying it's impossible.

"So, what did you think?" Ike is sitting at the nursing station, feet up on the desk, file in lap while Jeff is leaning against the wall. Both look incredibly interested in whatever I have to say.

"Did you guys listen in?" I mainly drive this question toward Jeff, knowing Ike wouldn't do that.

"He wanted to." Ike rats him out, but I figured anyway. The guy is a heavy walker, and he didn't bother to hide his elephant stomps as he paced the hallway.

"Farmer Joe is gone. Will you see to it?" I direct this to Ike, ignoring Jeff completely as I take Joe's file and write down some notes.

Ike pushes himself to his feet and gets to work. He knows I'll share whatever details I want with him later.

"Well?" Jeff doesn't seem to take the hint. He's now beside me, trying to read the notes I'd written from Farmer Joe's confession.

I place my hand over the top of the notebook. "You can ask me one question. Only one. I'll make sure the Warden knows I took the confession, so you get your money and hunting trip. I want half of what you shoot, deal?"

It's a tall ask, but if the kid wants to reap the benefits, he'll make the deal with me.

"I can do that," he says, nodding. He takes his time, thinking about his question, which I'm surprised about. I figured he'd have a million of them and just ask whichever came first.

"What happened to his boys?"

Not did he have boys, but what happened…interesting.

"What do you think happened?"

A wide smirk covers Jeff's face. "He fed them to the pigs, didn't he? That son of a bitch actually did it, didn't he?" His right hand slaps his leg with a smack. "I knew it. I knew the rumors were true."

I don't answer. I really don't feel like I need to. I head into my office, close the door and do the one thing I've wanted to do since entering Farmer Joe's room.

I take out my bottle from the desk drawer and inhale, driving all shit scent from my nose.

HENRY

PATIENT 523

CHAPTER
ONE

I have a secret.

It's not just 'my' secret either. Everyone who works at the Asylum knows about this tasty little piece of news, and we've all agreed to keep it between us.

You probably want to know what it is...and I'll probably tell you, but not right now.

First, I want to introduce you to another patient of mine. He's part of the secret, if you must know.

Let's call him Henry.

Henry is a little...different. He's been here since the early seventies and caused quite the commotion too. Many folks thought he should have been sent to the regular prison where he was sentenced to death. Still, his lawyers were able to get him admitted into an 'institution,' which then transferred him here.

This happens more than you'd expect.

Henry, he's been with us ever since.

Henry isn't like the others here. At least, he likes to think he's different. He claims to be one hundred percent sane, like you and me. He swears that all the drugs we keep him on have dulled his brain, making him appear...like he has issues.

Truth be told, a lot of them say that.

Trust me when I tell you, no one is here at the Asylum, unless they deserve to be. If anyone attempts to tell you otherwise, they're lying to you.

Henry's been on my floor for a total of three days. He's nearing the end, for sure, but he's got some life left in him still.

I finish my preliminary rounds to find Ike sitting at the nursing station, feet up on the desk, arms relaxed behind his neck.

"Gonna be a quiet night, boss," he says, twirling a toothpick in his mouth.

I knock his feet off the desk, then perch on the edge.

"Guess that means we can tackle the list." I nudge my head toward the page tacked to the wall. The department head wants a full clean on the ward, even though we just did one a few months ago. Typically housekeeping hires temp workers to do the work, but the powers that be insist on tightening the belts a little.

If you ask me, they're scrimping and saving to make sure they all get their bonus money at the end of the year.

"Tackle but not complete," Ike says, leaning forward to read through the list. "Last time, the night shift ended up doing all of it."

"Not quite." This has been a regular grumble and only added to the whole division between the day and night shifts.

The toothpick in his mouth stills as he stares at me. "At least a solid eighty percent of it."

His argument is sound, I'll give him that. My shift tends to get the short end every time. "I'll talk to the day shift head," I say, which earns me a grunt from Ike before he pops to his feet.

"How's Henry?" He asks.

"Watching his favorite show. Golden Girls."

Ike brought in a DVD collection of Golden Girls for Henry, and it's been on repeat for the past three days.

"He's been in quite the mood, have you noticed? He told me he thinks maybe he's ready for round three."

This isn't the first time Henry has been on my floor. He was here a few years ago after catching pneumonia. No one thought he'd make it then, but he proved us all otherwise.

I remember chatting with him once when he was here the first time, asking how he felt, now that his life was coming to an end.

"This isn't the end, Jack. You, of all people, should know that."

I didn't think much of his comment. I guess I figured he meant there's more to life than death, more to live for after this passing.

I'm not sure if Henry believes in heaven or hell or reincarnation or what, but that's what I thought he'd meant.

I was wrong.

Three days later, the doctors deemed him fit enough to head back down to his regular floor.

A few days ago, when I came on shift and saw him being wheeled into an empty room, I'd been a little surprised and caught off guard. I usually get a heads up when someone is being brought up.

The Asylum's head warden, named funny enough, Thomas Warden, even accompanied Henry.

That doesn't happen often.

I can count on one hand the number of times Warden has walked alongside a patient as they came onto my floor.

If he does, there's a reason.

Finding out that reason is always important. Out of everyone in the Asylum who plays games, Warden is the master.

"Henry here, he's a special one," Warden says to me. "Make sure you take care of him, okay, Jack?"

Warden and I, we're on good terms. We've been known to suck back a few pints or two down at the pub, and he's even had me over to his fancy place for dinner. His wife cooks a mean rack of lamb.

"You got it, Warden. Henry and I will get along fine, don't you worry. His last days will be some of his best." I make sure Henry sees my wink, and I catch a slight smile on his face beneath his oxygen mask.

Warden pulls me to the side after Henry has gone into his room.

"In the mood for a good hunt, Jack? Why not join me this

weekend? We'll eat what we kill, have a feast that ends with a good whiskey. What do you say?"

The grounds around the Asylum are rich in deer, rabbits, and pheasant. This wouldn't be the first time Warden and I have gone hunting. It won't be the last, either.

We've got a tradition between the Warden and me. I take a confession he's interested in, he invites me hunting, and I share the story over some whiskey after his wife has gone to bed.

"Sounds like a plan."

Warden gives me a solid handshake before he leaves my floor with a whistle.

The past couple of days, I've made sure to poke my head into Henry's room to see how he's doing. Right before I leave, he tells me the same thing: "I'm not ready yet."

Fair enough. I put my offer out there, unsure if he'd take it. Most of the time, I know if a patient will accept what I bring to the table, but you can never fully be sure with Henry.

I mentioned he's an odd duck, didn't I? No, I think what I said was, he's a little different.

Let me explain…

CHAPTER
TWO

I wait a bit before I head in to see Henry.

I'm going to be an ass, but it'll bring a smile to his face.

The first thing I do is warm up a mini frozen pizza and slap it on a plate. While it's still hot and has that greasy smell to it, I hike down to Henry's room and stand in the doorway.

His eyes are closed, but he raises his head about an inch from the pillow, that big snout of his, sniffing the air.

"Grease. Mass-manufactured. Gonna taste like cardboard."

I take a bite and ignore his words even though he's right. It tastes like shit, but what can you expect from microwaved pizza?

"If you're wanting the good stuff, ask Mario down in the kitchen. He'll make you my signature pizza, Jack. He's the only one I shared my recipe with."

Henry comes from a long line of Italians. He claims his family used to own the oldest pizza joint in Chicago before they got shut down, thanks to his arrest. Regardless if his claim is true or not, I'm sure they reopened in no time flat, with a few changes to their setup.

"I can't believe you trusted someone like that." I set the plate I'm holding down on the dinner tray in Henry's room. Not sure why it's here, the man won't be eating anything. All his nutrients are fed via intravenous now.

"They wouldn't let me in the kitchen." Henry finally opens his eyes. "Life is about compromises, Jack. If I wanted good pizza, I had to find someone I could trust with the recipe."

"How'd you pick Mario?"

"He proved himself trustworthy."

I wait to see if he'll say more, but he doesn't. I lean back against the wall, arms crossed over my chest.

"You'd think they'd want someone who could actually cook, to work in the kitchens," Henry says, giving his head a slight shake. "When I first arrived, the food was barely edible. Soups that tasted more water than anything else, pasta that was always overcooked, and I swear the only seasoning they used was salt."

I'm not surprised to hear this, Henry's been here a long time, and most prisons aren't known to have five-star dining.

"You could have requested to work in the kitchens," I say.

He laughs, albeit a very pitiful, painful laugh.

"Like I said, they wouldn't let me in there. Didn't trust me, I guess." His eyes sparkle, and I give a slight chuckle.

"Do you blame them?"

Henry here has a...history. I know a little of his past, mainly from what I'd read in his file and online. Add to that the whispered rumors of mob executions, and well...nothing would surprise me.

"I'm not like that, Jack. All those things you've heard about me, they're not true."

"Is that right?"

The look on Henry's face has me questioning if anything or everything I've heard could be true.

Does he look like a cold-blooded killer?

Do I think him capable of destroying lives and committing unspeakable acts?

Yes, yes, I do.

Just because someone looks innocent doesn't mean they are. Looks are deceiving, don't let anyone tell you otherwise.

"I know no one believes me. Everyone thinks I'm something

I'm not. Even you, I see it in your eyes. That deal of yours…I have a condition."

A condition? I'll admit, I'm a little surprised. I can count on one hand the number of people who've tried to pull this stunt with me.

He should know better. My deals are non-negotiable.

I push myself away from the wall and yawn.

"That's not how this works, sorry, Henry. I've got some rounds to do, but I'll be sure to check in later, okay?"

This is my ward.

He's on my turf.

He doesn't get to call the shots, and the only game we play is the one where I determine the rules.

"What? Don't want to hear what I have to say? Come on, Jack…"

My hand is on the door, ready to open it fully, but I pause.

"It's a harmless request, I promise. I'll take you up on the deal, I'll tell you my story, the real story, for one small favor."

What would Henry ask for? I'll admit, I'm intrigued. He wants a favor…something other than an easy and painless death.

"I want to die with the smell of pizza surrounding me. Do you think that'd be possible, Jack? Mario promised he'd make me my signature dish as a farewell gift, but I need you to tell him when. That's all."

That was it? A request for pizza? Hell…if the guy wanted a pizza farewell party, all he had to do was say the word.

"I'll think about it," I tell him before closing the door behind me as I leave his room.

CHAPTER
THREE

Word has gotten out about Henry's presence being on the floor. Every patient I see asks me how he's doing.

I tell them all the same thing. "About the same as you." Everyone here is waiting to die, so what else could I say?

Everyone knows Henry, and most everyone likes him, too. He's not a hard man to like. He's amicable, listens well, always has a story to tell, and enjoys a good belly laugh. Fuck, that sounds like a bio you'd find on a dating site.

When you think of a mob boss, Henry isn't it, which I think was or is the point.

Mob boss, do you need me to say it again?

Henry came into the Asylum with the whispered warnings of his past.

If someone says it's true, does it make it so?

Just because he was taken off the streets and away from his crew didn't change who he was, not deep down. I've heard the stories of the men who sought out his favor since he's been here...and not just about other inmates, either.

Why do you think Warden is so interested in him?

He's had every Warden, every guard, every doctor and inmate in his pocket at one point or another.

Even me.

Surprised you with that one, didn't I?

Yep, back in the day, shortly after I'd first arrived, I paid a visit to Henry. I'd heard that if I wanted to earn a name, if I wanted to be respected while here, he was the man to help with that.

Ever heard of the Chicago Outfit? Ever watched Goodfellas? Remember the presence those guys had? I thought I'd be scared shitless to talk with Henry. I thought he was bigger than life, that with one look, he'd have me shitting my pants.

I was wrong.

When I walked into his room, he pulled me into a hug, with a huge shit-eating grin on his face, and welcomed me to the family. He asked me all sorts of questions; about my career, what I wanted to do, why I became a nurse.

Then we talked food. If there's one thing Henry loved to discuss, it is food.

Henry and Chef were best friends, from what I'm told. They'd pour over the recipe books from the library, discuss ways to marinate meat and even taught classes a few nights a month to the staff.

The only time they ever entered the kitchen was under supervision and never with another inmate as a threesome. You'll find out why later.

I have always found their relationship…interesting.

My first meeting with Henry ended with a piece of advice. It's one I've never forgotten either.

"The only time you ever see a person's true character, who they really are, is right before they die. Anytime you judge a person before seeing their true self, you're robbing yourself of an opportunity. Don't wait for death to look; you're smart, I can see it. You have the gift to see who a person truly is, even before they're willing to admit it. Use that to your advantage, and you'll do fine here."

He wasn't wrong.

Since then, I have made an effort not to judge a person based on hearsay, or what's in their files, or even due to rumors that tend to spread like wildfire through the Asylum.

I judge them based on my interaction with them and in those moments when they understand death is close.

Back at my desk, I pick up the phone and dial the kitchen.

"Is Mario on shift today?" I ask one of the guards, who answers. He places me on hold for about a minute.

"This is Mario."

It's everything I can do not to laugh. I wasn't sure what I expected, but a high-pitched, almost child-like voice wasn't it. Actually, the voice could be a clone for the Luigi voice used on the Mario games.

I wonder if Ike knows about this? He's a huge SuperMario fan.

"This is Jack."

There's silence on the phone for a total of four seconds.

"I've been wondering when you'd call. He's ready for his last meal, is he?"

"I'm thinking we'll have a pizza party to celebrate," I say. "Can I trust you to take care of it?"

There's a sharp inhale. "No one has trusted me like he has. For him, I'll do anything. When do you need it by?"

I look at the clock and give him a deadline. Do I think Henry will be dead by then? No. The goal is to have the pizza arrive while he's telling me his story. Not before and definitely not after.

Henry did me a solid all those years ago when I first started here. The least I can do is return the favor.

CHAPTER
FOUR

Ike's sipping coffee after I hang up the phone.

"Holy hell, have you heard his voice?" I grab a cup from the cupboard and pour what's left of the coffee in it.

He pulls out his phone, plays with it for a minute before he plays a recording.

"Okie Dokie, it's only me. Pick up the phone."

"Shut up, that sounds exactly like him." I grab his phone and play it again.

"I know, right? I met the guy outside a few years ago during a smoke break. Cracks me up every time he opens his mouth." Ike pockets his phone with a grin. "I use that ring tone for my parents."

I take a sip of the coffee and immediately dump the rest out. "How can you drink that shit? It's not even warm."

"Who said I'm drinking coffee?" Ike's one brow rises as he takes another sip.

I should check his cup. I technically have to check his cup now, but I'm going to ignore his comment instead. Officially drinking during a shift is prohibited, but I like to keep a bottle of Scotch in my desk drawer for those *hard* days. And by hard days, I mean days I lose a patient.

Just because I'm known as Death Angel doesn't mean it's an easy task.

"So let me guess, Mario is making Henry a pizza?" Ike sets his cup down on the counter and pats his stomach while smiling. "I can't wait. Ever since I found out he has the secret recipe, I've been trying to get him to let me taste it. You do realize he only makes this for Henry and no one else?"

This time it's my turn to smile. "Call me your fairy godfather. Mario will be making enough for all of us."

"Shut up." He slaps my shoulder with strength. "Hopefully, there won't be any *secret* ingredients." The smirk on his face has my stomach do a quick roll, but I'm not about to admit that to him.

The secret ingredients Ike's hinting at are hopefully part of Henry's story he'll tell me. The papers were full of stories, but no one was sure if they were truthful or fables meant to scare the masses.

Considering how close Henry and Chef were...it wouldn't surprise me if the stories were real.

One thing I'll have to keep in mind with Henry if his story is true: once in the mob, always in the mob.

I leave Ike thinking about the pizza we'll be enjoying later and head to my office. I keep a particular journal in there, the one where I record all the stories. I then grab my chair and start pulling it behind me.

The wheels squeak as I head toward Henry's room. It's still early enough that most everyone is awake, and a few call out as I pass their doors.

"Make this passage a gentle one."

"Will you tell me a bedtime story tonight, Jack?"

I shake my head, ignoring them all.

"Knock, knock," I say as I stop at Henry's door. He doesn't hear me. His head faces the opposite wall, but his chest still moves.

I could leave, let him sleep, but then he turns his head to me with a slight smile.

"Just resting my eyes, Jack. Come on in," he says.

"I called down to the kitchen and chatted with Mario," I tell him as I take my seat.

His eyes light up. "Is that so?"

"While we wait, I thought maybe you'd be ready to tell me a story." I open my notebook and turn to a blank page, pen poised, and wait.

CHAPTER
FIVE

HENRY TO JACK

Sure, sure, I've got a story to tell. But are you going to believe me?

You hear this all the time, don't you, Jack? Everyone wanting to tell you their story and swearing it's the real one.

That's what you want, isn't it? The real story?

No? You don't care? Nah, I don't believe that. I get you say it, that you want any story, as long as it's not been told before, but come on, Jack, tell me the truth.

Do you really care if it's real or not?

Huh. That's what I figured. You do care. Thought so.

Well, I've got a story, and it's the real one. Ain't never told another soul. I promised I'd take this secret to the grave with me, but seeing how the grave is here, I've changed my mind.

I'd like to tell you my story, Jack. It doesn't matter now if it's kept a secret. Doubt anyone is left for the truth to affect.

So, I guess the question I need an answer to first is this: will you believe me?

It's important, Jack.

CHAPTER
SIX

HENRY

I grew up in a traditional Italian home.

There were seven of us in the house. Mamma, Pops, Nonna and Nonno, me, my brother and my uncle. My familia. Families stick together, stay together, work together and die together. Nonno, my grandfather, he died when I was young, a heart attack at the pizzeria one night. I don't remember much about him. When he came home at nights, my brother and I were often sent to bed. He was loud, authoritative, and had a firm hand.

I remember someone once saying Nonno was like royalty in Chicago, and his funeral proved it. I don't remember much about it, I think I fell asleep in the pew, but the church was packed. Mass went on for so long, but the food after, ahhh...that I remember. It was a party in Nonno's honor. Everyone was there, families from the block, those in high places with drivers and everything - I used to think it was because of his pizza.

That was only partially true.

Mamma was strong, kill-with-a-look, and loved-with-a-spoon kind of mother. She was the best cook, no one beat her cooking, no one. When I say she loved with a spoon, it was wooden and was discolored from sitting in spaghetti sauce for too long.

The best memories I have of her were in the kitchen. She was always in the kitchen - her and Nonna. Bread, pasta, sauces, mouth-watering baking...do you know, I can still smell that kitchen? The spices, the earthy bread smell... I'm taking that memory to the grave with me.

I always wanted to learn to cook. Mamma, she said it was in my blood. I used to stand beside her when I was just knee-high, on a stool, stirring the sauces, grinding the garlic, licking the bowls.

She taught me, us, how to cook, how to create dishes that soothed a soul and shared the secrets of a heart. We would make fresh tomato sauce, cream, and butter sauces. Add a little parsley or basil, a hint of parmesan... I'd give anything to taste her cooking again.

All my life, I was happiest in a kitchen. Give me some fresh ingredients, flour, a pot of water and I'm in heaven. The hardest thing for me to get used to when I first came here was not having kitchen access.

Did you know it took me seven years before they let me in there? Seven long years.

They took me at night, when everyone was sleeping, and told me I had two hours. Oh, Jack, the things I made in those two hours...

They say there are no lies in the kitchen.

It's true. It's the only place I've ever felt my true self.

Those late nights, I'd often find Warden there, waiting for me. He'd be sitting there, stool pulled up to the large centre metal island, with bags full of fresh ingredients, and we'd talk, swap stories, over fresh spaghetti or gnocchi or even pizza.

Ahh...pizza. That's in my bones. In my blood.

My pops, he ran the family pizza joint after Nonno died. It's been in the family for years, his grandfather started it as a classic pizza place, and that's how we ran it too. He left the house in the early hours and came home in time for dinner. His brothers ran the place at night. When Pops came home, we had a revolving back door; friends, neighbors - everyone and anyone would drop by.

Our house was loud. Boisterous. Full of energy and life. It wasn't a big place. It was older, run-down, a mess, but it was home. Everything you'd expect an Italian American family to be, that was us.

My parents fought hard, loved hard, and raised us to be hard.

Don't get me wrong - I had a good childhood, you know? Compared to others, it was good.

I lived in that house for most of my life. I was twenty-two before I moved out. When I was twenty-two, my life changed in ways I wasn't prepared for.

You know, living at home with my family, we had a good life. It wasn't easy, but it wasn't hard either. My parents taught me to live hard, love hard, and expect hardship to be part of my life. They taught me that it wasn't what I did with my life that mattered, but how I lived my life.

Did I honor my family? Did I put our community first? Did I watch out for those who needed the help?

If I wasn't someone people came to in the hard times, then I was living my life wrong.

Even now, all my years here, that's how I try to guide my days.

It hasn't always been easy, and I'm not going to lie, my name brings about expectations, some I've had no choice but to meet. It's hard living up to a heritage, you know? It's hard living up to a name, to a legacy. But, that's all I ever wanted with my life: to be given the chance to live up to that legacy and make my family proud.

No matter what it's taken.

CHAPTER
SEVEN

HENRY TO JACK

That garbage you'd brought in earlier, that pizza? What was that?

A trick? A joke? A mean reminder of what I'd lost?

That wasn't fair, man.

Just wait, Jack...just wait. You haven't had pizza till you've tasted my pizza. It might not be by my hands, but Mario, he has the gift, and I've taught him well.

I'm sure you've heard the stories about the Warden and me, right? How he'd wake me up in the middle of the night, lead me into the kitchen and we'd chat over fresh gnocchi? In the beginning, he'd have a guard or two escort me, but over the years, he came himself. A nice touch, don't you think?

At first, waters were being tested - could I be trusted? Was I loyal? What did I have to offer?

I'm pretty sure I passed every single test that came my way. Even the hard ones. Especially the hard ones.

I know you've heard the rumors, Jack. Rumors of things I've done, of the hold I have on certain guards, patients...do you believe them?

No, don't answer that. Let me live with the fallacy that you go with your gut, that you trust only your instincts, and that you don't believe everything you're told.

Not all the rumors about me are true.

CHAPTER
EIGHT

HENRY

I only had one dream in my life: to run the pizza shop with my brother.

It might not seem like a lot to make pizza day in and day out and be responsible for my family and my community's well-being.

But, the day I was handed the keys, when I saw the pride in my father's eyes…it was like Saint Peter himself blessing me.

My father didn't look at me like that too often. No matter how hard I tried to earn his praise.

If there was pride, it was typically given to my brother, but on that day, when he handed me the keys…the whole family was thrilled.

Taking over the shop, it was a legacy passed down, you know? From father to son, keeping the business, the thing that provided for your family, alive. It was all I ever wanted, all I ever dreamed about.

Following in the family business, walking in the footsteps of the greats… it's a heavy burden.

It wasn't just pizza and pasta. It wasn't just starting the ovens, mixing the dough for the pizza, cutting all the produce…it was being given the trust for the recipes, keeping the name and reputation alive.

It wasn't easy. In fact, it was quite brutal.

I had a brother, I've mentioned him a few times now. Did you know we were twins?

Running that pizza shop, that was our legacy.

All our lives, up to that point, we'd been glued to the hip. We did everything together. We played on the same teams, sat beside each other in class, went on dates together, hung out with the same crowd. We were inseparable.

My brother...he looked out for me. Took care of me. Protected me. He always said I might have a head for business, but not for life. I never understood what that meant, not for a long time. Our lives had been planned for us - we were going to run the shop together, but then, trouble happened.

One night he was by my side, and the next night I was told he was dead.

I don't like to talk about my brother much.

It's not that I didn't love him, because I did. It's not that I don't miss him, because I do.

But after being my protector for most of my life, he suddenly became a danger...to me, and to my family.

I can't pinpoint the exact time this happened. Maybe when we were sixteen? Definitely by the time we turned eighteen.

We eventually hung out with different crowds. My friends were...stable, I guess you could say. His friends...well, they were tough.

As kids, we were inseparable.

As adults, it was better not to be associated with him.

By the time I turned twenty-one, we'd gone in such different directions that it was safe to say I didn't know my brother at all anymore.

While I spent my free hours at the shop, helping out, being dependable, he was doing the opposite. He rarely came into the shop unless it was to grab food or *meet* with someone about some deal that would *benefit* the family.

My father and him, they would argue, fight. Came to fists often.

My mother and him, she would cry, beg. Always smother him with hugs.

Me...I was left to the side. I grew to be quiet. I focused on the food, on learning how to cook with heart, changing business practices to bring in more money. I wouldn't say I was ignored... but I wasn't the problem child, so I didn't need as much attention.

I know what you're thinking...my brother was a drug addict or sold drugs to addicts. No, he was smarter than that. He made himself indispensable - to the druggies, to the dealers, to the distributors. He made a name for himself, one that continued to go until the Chicago Outfit caught wind of him.

You know about the Chicago Outfit, right? I don't need to explain that, right?

Once he became known to them, our world as we knew it changed.

My parents would argue about his involvement with the Outfit for hours, evening after evening. My brother turned a deaf ear, not listening to how he ruined our name, destroyed our legacy.

He would meet me late at night, at the pizza shop just before I'd close. He had a strategy, a plan, one I didn't understand.

He begged me to trust him. So I did.

How could I not? We were living different lives, but we were the same person.

We still are. That's my secret.

CHAPTER
NINE

HENRY TO JACK

What? You don't believe me, Jack?

I'm telling you the truth.

There's a bond between twins. Surely you believe that?

Did you know that identical twins even share the same DNA? It's true. We were formed from the same sperm into the same egg. We are the same, regardless of how different our lives are, regardless of our choices. Put us in a lineup, and you won't tell the difference. Take our blood, watch our mannerisms… there's no difference.

What? No… you're wrong. Identical twins are just that…identical.

I don't believe you, Jack. Back then, the police couldn't tell us apart, and it would be the exact same today.

I don't believe things have progressed so much that you can tell us apart now, even by our blood.

What happened to my brother? I'm getting to that.

He's the reason I'm here. He's the reason for the secret. For the lies. For the deceit. He's the reason my family was destroyed.

At the time, he looked like our savior.

He was a devil in disguise. I know you want to know what he did, why he changed and placed our family in the position he did…but that's his story. Not mine.

Do you know, if he were here now, if I could see him again, all the past, every vile thing he did...it would be erased and forgiven.

That's what families do, don't they? Forgive?

I'd give anything to see my brother one last time, to offer that forgiveness. I think it would give him peace.

I know it would for me.

Especially after all he did.

CHAPTER
TEN

HENRY

The day we announced my brother's death, our whole lives changed.

We were no longer the same. I was no longer the same. Our family dynamic altered...and not for the better.

Before, others in our community would come to us for help, calling us angels. After, it was like we were the demons.

Dying, that had been his plan. His way of making our family stronger, carry more influence. Everyone was against it, but he gave us no choice.

He gave me no choice.

He told me of his plan days in advance, but I didn't think he would go through with it.

Dead, he offered us more protection. Alive, he was just a liability.

No one believed him.

We should have, because he was right.

Before his death, the police were always around, not just to our home but also our community, the shop...he was always getting tossed into jail, threatened, and beaten up. My father was humiliated, having to save him, beg for protection... I'd never seen him so low before.

Our family, we were always on the top, in the know, but thanks to my brother's actions, we'd fallen low, held no sway, no authority anymore.

My brother's death...it changed all that.

You think you know the mob.

Everyone thinks they understand how it works, the rules played, the lifestyle, the danger. All because of movies and actors and rumors.

Unless you are in the Family, you have no understanding.

It's a dangerous world, and as much as I thought I knew that, I didn't truly understand what it meant until after my brother faked his own death.

I mentioned our lives changed, and they did.

For the worst and for the best.

CHAPTER
ELEVEN

HENRY TO JACK

Oh, you caught that, did you. The fact my brother faked his own death. Yeah, you heard that right.

Take that in, Jack.

Now let me ask another question: If my brother is still alive...then why am I in here?

Family is everything. Family is all. The Family never turns their back on their own - no matter what.

The Family creed is the foundation for the Italian mob, even here in the United States of Bloody America.

When it came to the Order, our family grew until it wasn't just about our small community anymore.

When family is the basis for everything you do, then you'll understand why I'm in here, and he's out there.

Did I do the things I was charged with?

Did I maim people and force them to eat their own fingers or ear lobes?

Did I order the lives of over fifty men to their death?

Was I the mastermind of an organization housed in the belly of a pizza shop?

Maybe. Maybe not.

CHAPTER
TWELVE

HENRY

Working in the shadows has benefits, as we quickly realized after my brother faked his death.

With him dead, the police visits stopped. That was huge, especially for my parents. Mom started smiling again, she slept better at night, and my Pops was in the shop more often, helping out, greeting customers, and such.

They became different people overnight.

They became the parents I remembered growing up.

My brother, just because he was out of sight, didn't mean he was out of mind. He set up shop in the back of the pizzeria, and thanks to him, our shop started seeing the black in the books, rather than always being in the red.

Being dead certainly did have its benefits.

Two years after his supposed death, we were able to buy out the vacant shop next to us. We busted out a few walls, increased our dining and kitchen space, and transformed a section of the back into an office of sorts for my brother. It's where he conducted business, and by business, I mean...where he took care of things.

My brother became a King in death.

He'd made a deal with the devil himself - and by devil, I mean the big kingpin, who ran the mob in Chicago. Tony. I don't need to tell you his full name, you know it all ready.

I won't bore you with the details of how he accomplished this, but his pathway was paved in bodies and minions who knew not to piss him off. Blind obedience is the best kind of obedience, especially if people knew they could lose an eye if they sought to challenge the Family.

Me...I stayed out of things. I wanted nothing to do with that life, and as far as I was concerned, the less I knew, the better.

My brother tried to get me to join him, but my focus was the pizzeria, and he eventually respected that.

Eventually.

That's not to say, at times, the two businesses didn't intermix. Sometimes I'd have to stay late to keep the shop open - for appearance's sake, of course.

The first time this happened, I'd closed shop and headed upstairs only to have to return about an hour later to retrieve a file or something.

I found my brother and one of his partners in the kitchen, making a pizza.

Now, normally this wouldn't be an issue. This was as much his shop as mine, or anyone else's in the family.

The issue was the mess his partner was making in the kitchen while waiting for the pizza to bake.

I can't stand a mess. It's truly the one thing that will push me over the edge.

Nothing was clean. The counters were covered in sauce, fresh sausage taken out of the casing, and the cheese...it was everywhere.

So much disrespect, and I couldn't handle it.

Despite my brother telling me to head back upstairs, I shouldered my way past him and his business partner and started to clean things up.

It didn't take me long to realize three things:

One - there was someone else in the room with us, mouth taped shut, hands wrapped in a bloody cloth.

Two - the sauce on the counter wasn't tomato-based. It was blood.

Three - the casing from the sausage was actually skin.

Any guesses what happened next? Why don't I just tell you, huh?

They made the man eat this small personal pan pizza, a pizza where the main ingredient was meat mixed with his own fingers.

I never asked what the point they were attempting to get across was or what the man's crime was, but acts of strength like that were what paved the way for my brother to become as important as he was.

Even dead, he had a voice, and that voice was loud enough to make a difference in our community.

That might have been the first time I became aware of how the pizzeria was used in his business dealings, but it certainly wasn't the last.

CHAPTER
THIRTEEN

HENRY TO JACK

Did the police know he was dead?

Hmmm...good question. They could never prove otherwise, which is why most of my brother's alleged crimes were placed on my shoulders.

Did it bother me?

Did what bother me? You're going to have to be a bit more specific than that, Jack.

Having my reputation ruined?

My life destroyed?

Being sent here for crimes HE committed?

Family is family.

Him being outed and placed in jail would have destroyed everything he'd worked for. Our community was safe, finally. Yes, he was the one who brought the danger to us, but once he saw the error of his ways, he fixed that mistake.

How did he fix it? Come on, Jack, haven't I been clear enough?

My brother received a Hail Mary from the one in charge. He took a deal, saved his life, made sure our community was safe. He did what he needed to do for big Tony to not kill him and destroy our family.

The deal? I thought I'd made that clear with the finger pizza story. No?

He took care of issues for big Tony. He had to prove himself, and I guess he did. I didn't ask how, and I certainly didn't want to know what happened.

The less I knew, the better.

All that mattered is he took care of what he'd done to our family and our community. Rather than continuing to destroy us and our name, he saw the error of his ways and changed things for the better.

If it meant a few people had to die for that to happen, so be it.

What? You don't approve?

Just because you might have clear boundaries of what is right and wrong, doesn't mean those are my boundaries.

I was raised that Family is all.

Once my brother took that deal, our small community became part of La Familia. Which meant, even though it was my brother who had the deal, his responsibility became mine too.

I gave my all for La Familia. If you protect the Family, the Family protects you. That's just how it works.

That's what defines my right and wrong.

Don't make the mistake, however, that I'm like my brother. I'm nothing like him.

CHAPTER
FOURTEEN

HENRY

It's hard having your dreams stolen from you.

It's hard when those dreams you've worked hard for are crushed, when you're told to dream something else.

My only dream was to take over the pizzeria. To have it be so successful that it becomes a chain.

Turns out, my dreams didn't matter, not when it came to the Family.

Becoming a chain would have cast too many eyes on us. Becoming a chain would have had too many people involved, too many people who might find out my brother wasn't dead.

So I killed that dream and made another one. If I couldn't have a chain, then I sure as hell wanted my pizzeria to be famous. I worked hard, and eventually, we expanded in size, had more customers, but kept our circle small.

Let me get back to what being an identical twin means to my brother and his business dealings: If someone saw him in the kitchen, or even outside of it - like around town and whatnot, they'd think it was me.

We'd often have catch-up sessions late at night once we were alone.

I can't tell you the number of times he'd fill me in on whom he saw or spoke with - so that I wouldn't be caught unaware.

That wasn't the only thing we'd do to make sure no one could tell the difference between him and me.

There was one time when he stumbled into the kitchen late at night with a knife cut across his cheek.

Being his double had its ramifications. After cleaning him up, sewing the cut shut, we then made sure I had the same scar, right here, on my cheek, too.

Anyone on his crew, and they were only a few, could always tell the difference between the two of us. I'm not sure how, but I never caught them mistaking me for him.

My brother was brutal. For anyone outside of his immediate circle, he was as cold as stone. Everyone was scared of him, and he was only scared of one: Big Tony.

Even my Pops grew fearful of him.

Me? I quickly realized the limits I could push. I kept my head down, focusing on the pizzeria and doing what I could to keep things running smoothly.

I stayed out of his business as much as I could. If he ever came into the kitchen late at night and gave me a look, I knew it was time to leave.

There were a few times I stayed, when I felt he needed support. He never said it, would never admit weakness, but I knew.

A twin always knows.

CHAPTER
FIFTEEN

HENRY TO JACK

Don't ask me about the dealings with the mob.

I know nothing about the organization, what Street Boss runs what, or anything else.

That's the one thing I asked when my twin told me what he'd done.

He promised to keep me clean as long as I promised to always have his back.

Well... I'm in here, aren't I? I'd say I had his back.

I'm serious, Jack. This confession has nothing to do with the mob and how it's run and what the government can pin on whom. This is about my secret, which I've told you.

Oh, I haven't been clear enough? Come on, Jack, you don't believe that. Even Warden knows the truth, even though he'll never come out and say it.

I was convicted of crimes I didn't commit.

I was sentenced to life in here, considered crazy for the time when I lost my marbles and tried to tell the truth, all for the safety of the Family.

While my brother remained employed by Big Tony, my parents, the Family, our community were safe.

There were no guarantees of that safety remaining if he got caught.

Do I believe I was played? Because I'm a twin? Sure, the thought has crossed my mind.

But played by whom? My brother or the one he worked for?

Possibly both. I overheard once that there was a plan if he ever got caught. It's why I had to get this cut on my cheek.

And it worked. I'm here. He's not.

Sure, I confessed...why wouldn't I? I'm guilty of hiding the truth. I'm guilty of turning a blind eye. I'm guilty of placing my Family first.

But am I guilty of the crimes I was charged with?

I didn't kill a single person, Jack.

I didn't maim or force anyone to eat their own appendages.

I certainly didn't threaten, pay off or disappear a single person.

That was all my brother.

Am I upset? Why would I be? Other than being taken away from my kitchen, I've played my part in taking care of our Family. That's what matters the most.

So why am I telling you this? Because I don't think it matters anymore if anyone finds out the truth. I've more than paid for his crimes, don't you think?

Am I worried you'll tell someone, and he'll get caught?

I'm not a fool, Jack. I know you'll be telling people - especially Warden, won't you?

As for my brother getting caught...if he hasn't been seen by now, why would he? I haven't heard from him in years. I haven't heard from anyone in the Family in years, to be honest. He's probably dead, for all I know.

CHAPTER
SIXTEEN

JACK

In terms of confessions, this one is pretty mild - I'll give you that.

Tell the truth, I expected more. More...details, maybe?

I was expecting stories, stories only imagined in those mob boss movies, you know? Stories that haven't yet been published about him and the Family. Stories that force me to step back and wonder if my safety is an issue even though he's dying only feet from me.

His secrets, though, they're nothing compared to the one I'm holding. The one I'm keeping from him.

What Henry doesn't know, the secret many of us in the Asylum know but are keeping from him, is this: His brother is here too. He has been for years.

He's in isolation, hidden away in a part of this monster of a building.

Only a specific few, those most trusted, have access to him.

Henry's brother - he's dangerous. He's kept sedated because that's the only way we guarantee our safety.

You think I'm exaggerating? When he first came here, he'd bit into the neck of one of the guards downstairs. That guard didn't live long.

I know what you're about to ask.

If Henry's brother is here, then why wasn't Henry released, right?

For one simple reason: he's not as innocent as he wants everyone to believe.

Henry may believe everything he's done was for his Family, to keep them safe and protected. Who knows, maybe deep down, that's the underlying reasoning for everything he'd done.

But it wasn't the only one.

Personally, I think Henry loved the thrill of that mob life. He became addicted to the danger, and yes, even though he may claim he never hurt anyone, I know for a fact he did.

He talks in his sleep, something I'm not sure he's aware of.

Remember...Henry and Chef were best friends, and you remember Chef, right?

The stories Henry has mumbled in his sleep...of the ears he's cut off, the tongues he's cut out, of the things he's forced people to eat on their pizzas... he's guilty, and he knows it.

MARY

PATIENT 983

CHAPTER
ONE

What's your relationship like with your mother?

I love mine. Mom treats me like her favorite son because that's exactly what I am. She cooks the best Sunday dinner and sends me home with tons of leftovers too. She spoils me, and I'm quite fine with that.

Throughout the years I've been here at the Asylum, we've had several women come to my floor - as I'm sure I've mentioned before.

Some are sweethearts. Some could be your next-door grandmother. Most of them aren't to be trusted with a plastic knife - given the opportunity, like a snide remark or a side glance, and they'll stick you with that knife in the eye socket faster than you could inhale a freshly made berry pie.

I'm not joking.

Patient 983 is a woman I've gotten to know over the years. She's interesting, fascinating as hell, and tonight I get her confession.

We're going to call her Mary. It's not her real name, obviously, but it fits, and as you read her story, you'll see why.

Mary has a mothering soul. She'll take anyone under her wing and mother the living soul out of them, if you get my drift. She claims her only goal in life was to mother the lost, and she's done precisely that...even to the lost here within these walls.

In fact, there's a group of girls down on the fifth floor that live in a perpetual state of childhood. For their mental health, remaining young seems to be a safe place for them, despite how old their bodies may be. They stay in a series of rooms that we call the nursery, and there are about seven of them in total.

Mary was their chaperon, I guess you could call her. I'm not sure what they'll do now that she's here on my floor.

She's dying from cervical cancer that has progressed to her bowls and continues to spread. Cancer is such a rebellious, disgusting disease. I can't count on my hands anymore how many patients I've watched wither away from it.

In my opinion, Mary has had enough suffering.

I've spoken to her about the deals I make, offered it to her, and she said she'd think about it.

That surprised me.

I figured she'd jump at the chance, most do. I'm not dumb, I know almost everyone comes here hoping to get a deal offer from me.

I don't want to hear everyone's so called confessions. Just the ones I think haven't been told yet.

Mary, she honesty is a sweetheart. She's soft spoken, mild mannered, and has the best sayings too.

She kind of reminds me of my mom, truth be told. I'm not sure how Mom would feel about that, though. She's not the sharing type, even though she's constantly reminding me to treat these women as if they were her. I'm a good mother's son, but following that advice isn't always easy. Some women are catty and disgusting and very difficult to be around, and I figure, if I can't treat them like my mom, then it's better to let another staff member help them.

Hey, I'm not a saint. I never promised I would be, so don't judge me. Remember, the Asylum isn't a nice place to be. Come and work with me for a week, hell, you probably won't even last that long. Come work with me for a few days, and I promise you'll have nightmares you never thought possible to have.

And yet, I'm still here. Guess that says something about me, doesn't it.

CHAPTER
TWO

The floor is a little loud tonight.

As I walk along the hallways and poke my head into different rooms, there's one nurse that catches my attention.

I motion my hand to join me in the hallway after she's done with her rounds.

We have three females on the death floor tonight. That's a lot for us.

"Tonya, everything okay?" Her eyes are blazing bright red, and there are tear streaks down her cheeks. "What's going on?"

Tonya is relatively new. This is her second month here, and honestly, I'm surprised she's lasted this long.

She's a quiet girl with long brown hair tucked into a bun and the saddest brown eyes I've ever seen on someone. She's not the type to share a lot of information, personal or otherwise, as we're all finding out.

A few of the guys have hit on her, but it's like she's blind to their advances. Either that, or she knows what they're trying to do, and she could care less about it.

I have no idea if she has a boyfriend at home or even interested in men. Doesn't really matter, I guess. She reminds me of a butterfly with a broken wing, though, and I find myself drawn to her, wanting to protect her, make sure she's always okay.

See...I'm not that bad of a guy.

"Allison was telling me a story. She got too emotional and grabbed on to me." Tonya pulls back her sleeve, and her skin is all read. That's gonna bruise and bruise good.

"Why didn't you call for help?" I don't bother to mask the anger in my voice. She knows better. She's not a punching bag for our patients, and Allison should have been restrained.

"Why wasn't she cuffed? Did you let her off? She's restrained for a reason."

Tonya's head drops. "I know. I wanted to put a new pad around her wrist, I noticed the other slipped, and her skin is all red and cracked. I should have paid better attention."

"Yes, you should have. Or, at the very least, asked for help. Especially with her."

Allison isn't a patient that gets my deal. She's a mean old bugger, and in another life, she would have been a gnarly witch. When she dies, it's without me being present.

"I made a mistake. It won't happen again." She stares at the floor while she says this.

"Yes, you did, and yet it will," I say. I wait till she raises her gaze. "You'll make a lot of mistakes, and that's okay. That's how you learn. But the one thing you need to remind yourself every single shift is this: never underestimate those who come to this floor. Yes, they are here to die, but until their heart stops beating..." I let my voice trail off, not bothering to finish my sentence.

Tonya may have only been here for a little bit, but she's seen a lot. She's seen the crazy, the sane, and those in between. She's seen the kind of mind games some attempt to play, and she's had to be on guard not to get caught off guard.

She'll learn. I hope she sticks around long enough to become a good nurse because I know she has it in her.

"Have you checked in on Mary?" I ask.

Tonya nods. "She mentioned she's looking forward to a visit

from you tonight. She really is something, isn't she? She asked me to give her baby a bath before I left."

"That was nice of you. I'm on my way now to see her. If you need something, Ike is around, okay?" While I'm with Mary, hearing her final confession, I don't want to be disturbed if it can be helped.

I leave her to finish her rounds while I head to Mary's room.

Mary is in Bucket's room, the one that we painted and prettied up after she'd passed. I don't think I'll ever *not* think of this room as Buckets. That woman will always hold a special place in my heart. She was a wounded bird, abused and discarded in the worst ways possible.

Knock. Knock. I rap my knuckles on the door, easing it open with the toe of my shoe.

Mary lies in her bed, a frail little woman. She's wearing a thick cardigan that's wrapped tight around her frame, and in her arms is a doll.

That's her baby. She's never without one, carrying it with her all the time.

Mary looks up, the warmest of smiles on her face when she sees me.

"Jack! I'm so glad you're here. I was just about to tell Little Beatrice a story. Would you like to hear it too? I think this will be our last bedtime story. Beatrice is tired and ready for sleep."

CHAPTER
THREE

For someone about to die, Mary seems pretty happy.

It's like she's at peace with knowing the end is here, and it's just another thing to do.

Not many people are like that.

Some have a hard time letting go, saying goodbye. Others try to keep a stiff upper lip, pretend that death doesn't bother them. Then there are those just waiting for life to be over for them.

It's not many that embrace it with happiness. Especially when they're so sick.

Some patients have a few moments of complete clarity - in their mind, their heart, and their body. You'd swear they took a turn for the better, but I believe it's their body giving them some peace before that final breath.

That might be what's happening with Mary.

"Is there anything I can get for you first?" I offer.

"Oh, do we have some hot tea and maybe some cookies to nibble on? Our last bedtime snack should be a good one, don't you think, little Bea?" Mary's focus is on her doll, her fingers running her fingers across the perky cheeks.

When I first saw Mary holding a doll while during a group session years ago, I'd been shocked. I'd been young, relatively new, and stupid enough to approach her team and ask if it was healthy for her to be carrying a doll all day.

It didn't take me long to realize that everyone has their own hiccups in life. Some call them addictions, like the need for a smoker trying to quit to just hold an unlit cigarette between their fingers. Others classify them as talismans, like keeping a rabbit foot on a keychain for good luck, or how a Catholic might always finger a rosary.

For Mary, holding onto sanity meant carrying around a doll. This was her baby. She talked to it, bathed it, dressed it, fed it as if the doll were real. To her, I think it was.

When I was young and naive, I scoffed at the nurses who would help Mary bathe the baby, wash diapers, or even bring in baby clothes. It wasn't long, though, that whenever I found out Mary was hosting a birthday party for her baby, I made sure I brought a present.

"Could I get some fresh milk for lil' Bea, too?" She nods toward the bottle on the foot tray, and I give her a smile.

I hear the soft thump of footsteps coming down the hallway, so I grab the bottle and stand by the door.

"Tonya, do you have a moment?" I wait till she's a little closer. "I need a favor."

"If it's for Mary, I have all the time she needs," Tonya says, peaking into the room and giving Mary a smile.

I ask her to grab a fresh bottle and put together a tea tray, using cookies from the staff room, before returning to Mary's bedside.

"Are you going to sit down, Jack?" Mary asks, her soft voice so grandmotherly that it fills me with warm fuzzies.

I'm such a suck when it comes to certain patients of mine.

I pull out something that I'd stuck in my pocket earlier and lay it on the bed.

"Oh, what's that?" Mary tries to lift herself up so she can see. I hold the item up and wait for her reaction.

Knowing tonight would be our last talk, I stopped at a local children's store before heading into work tonight. I noticed that despite all the cute little outfits Mary had for her baby, the one thing she preferred to dress her in was a baby nightgown, the type that knotted at the bottom.

The nightgown I picked up is a soft pink color, and the fabric itself almost feels buttery. It knots at the bottom, and the neckline is covered in tiny white daisies.

"Oh, Jack. That is so beautiful. You always bring us the sweetest things," she basically coo's at me, and I find myself preening with pleasure.

Yep, I'm a suck.

I let Mary dress her baby in the new nightgown, and by the time Tonya arrives, we're all settled and ready for story time.

Tonya isn't alone when she arrives at the door.

"Hey, Ms. Mary," Ike says, his booming voice filling the room. "I brought you a warm blanket to go with your tea. Don't want those legs of yours getting cold now," he says.

While Tonya sets down the tray of tea and cookies, Ike gently places the warm blanket over Mary's body.

The audible sigh she gives is all Ike needs. "Only the best for my girl," he says.

"I told the girls downstairs to be nice to you, Ikey," Mary teases him with a nickname.

I want to laugh at the blush that rises to his face but avert my gaze instead. I'll have some fun with him later.

"Those girls are always nice to me, Ms. Mary. You didn't have to do that."

"Oh, but I did. They're going to struggle for a bit without me there, and if I didn't tell them in plain terms what I expect, well, it'd be chaos down there. Those nurses they have, they're all pushovers." She sounds harsh, but with the shake of her head and the way she smiles, I know she's not all that serious.

Those nurses, they definitely aren't pushovers, I don't know what Mary is talking about. Although, when it comes to her, most of us are, so...if they were soft, it's out of kindness for our Mary.

Without her presence down there, she's right, it will be chaotic for the first bit, but that team they have in the nursery, they'll handle it just fine, I have no doubt.

If need be, I'll send Ike down a few times to check in on them too.

"Was it hard, saying goodbye?" Tonya, still in the room with us, asks.

"Oh honey, by the time you reach my age, all you'll have done is say goodbye. Practice doesn't make perfect. It never gets easy; you just learn to handle your grief better."

CHAPTER
FOUR

MARY

I've lived a long life, and most of it within the very walls of this building.

I would say I've lived a good life, a life well-lived, even if most of it was here, in the Asylum. It doesn't matter what you do with your life, it's how you do it. So even if your existence seems sedentary, isolated, and unadventurous, if you do well with the life you've been given, then it's well-lived.

In fact, I'd say that the life I've lived since being here has been the best of my days. You find that hard to believe, I know, and yet, that's the gift you get with old age, the ability to look back and evaluate things.

My family has lived within these walls. They've also died within these walls. My daughters were my world, and every day I gave all of me to them.

That's a life well-lived, don't you think?

For a mother, that's what it's all about. Living for your children. Ensuring they have the best life, a full life, a life they can grab hold of with strength and understanding.

I've always heard that the worst thing that could happen to a mother is to outlive her children. I used to believe it too.

When I was naive and innocent, the idea of living without my baby...I couldn't fathom it. When I thought of the future, my future, my child, my children, they were always a part of that future.

I thought of birthdays and good night kisses, of bedtime prayers, and playing outside.

I imagined my babies with babies of their own, of discovering the love that they never knew possible.

I dreamed of holding those grand babies of mine and loving them with all of my being.

I never thought I'd end up alone.

I never imagined living past my child.

I never dreamed how painful loss truly feels.

I've often been asked if I'd do things differently, if I could have a do-over.

There's no such thing as do-overs.

Life is never that nice. Rarely are you given second chances, real second chances, but when you do, when they present themselves to you...you need to figure out if the strings attached are worth the price.

Everything Jack, everything comes with a price.

No, I'd never do things differently. For the simple reason that my life is richer because of my children, and if I didn't have the joy of having all of them in my life, I'd be a shell of the person I am today.

That's not a person I'd want to know.

I am a mother of many, and it's a mantle I wear with pride. The weight of this mantle is sometimes too much, but I've proven time after time that I'm stronger than I look.

Yes, cancer may have stolen this life, and the extra days I might have lived, but cancer has no control over my soul and spirit. It can destroy my body, but it will never conquer me.

The people I've met here, including you and Ikey, my life is that much richer, don't you think?

The life experiences I might not have had because I've been

here for so long… I've been able to live through you, through your stories. You're a great storyteller. Did you know that, Jack?

It's similar to being a reader - that addictiveness you feel to get lost within the pages of a book, within the characters of a story… you still live, through the experiences and words of others.

All my life, I've only ever wanted to be a mother. Even when I was younger, my Momma would tell me I had that mothering spirit about me. I was the oldest of thirteen, and she called me a natural. I had a good teacher. My Momma was everything you could want in a parent. She was strict when she needed to be but full of hugs and snuggles when she could. Daddy was hardly ever around. He worked on the trains, keeping the tracks working, and was rarely home. When he was, though, it was the best of days.

We were poor, didn't have much, and the more mouths to feed meant the less we had each year. I left home when I was sixteen. I feel in love with a drifter and followed him until the day he found out I was pregnant and left me alone in a small apartment.

God, I was so young back then. I thought love was love, that even in the worst of times, it would be the best of times, especially when a child was involved. But not to him. Having a child, to him, meant the end of his carefree days, and he didn't want that responsibility.

That was fine. He left me enough money to pay rent for a few months, and I had a job as a waitress at a local truck stop, so while I had a broken heart, I didn't have a broken spirit.

Even now, my spirit has never been broken. It's been damaged, for sure, but never destroyed. Not even when I was brought here because of my babies…not even then.

I have no regrets about loving those babies of mine. I want to be clear and upfront about that. I know others have judged me, called me a monster, and worse things, but I always had the purest of intentions. Always.

Every baby I took, I gave back…eventually.

All those babies, they were never mistreated. They had the best of everything I could offer, and they were surrounded with love. That's all they needed at that age.

I loved them with all of my being and recognized when I'd stepped over the line. Yes, I understand the damage I may have done to the original mothers of those children, but not all of them. There were a few that had no right being parents.

You know, I met one of those mothers here in the Asylum. I'm not sure if she knew who I was, but I recognized her. She wasn't here because of me, but it was because of me that she came to be here.

I wonder if the nurses ever knew? I always assumed they did, that they knew the history between us. They must have since we were never placed in the same groups. That's when I was moved to the nursery permanently - one of the best things to ever happen to me, by the way.

That woman? Yes, I'll tell you about her. She's part of my story, but before I get to her... there are other things you need to know first.

CHAPTER
FIVE

You never forget your first pregnancy.

It's the most amazing thing ever. That first time you feel the baby move, it's a miracle. I wish I'd had someone to share those firsts with, but I quickly realized that by not sharing, this miracle was all for me. I gave myself permission to be selfish with my baby, and I burned each experience into my brain, promising myself I would never forget.

I never did.

Working at the truck stop was one of the best experiences I'd ever had. I created my own little family within the staff there.

Big Mike was the chef, and he made sure I always had food to take home with me after my shift.

Lucy was the mother hen. She was in charge of the schedule and always made sure that I left my shift with a lot of tip money in my pocket.

Darwin was the owner. He'd sit at the end of the booth, keep an eye on the crowd, make sure people kept their hands to themselves, and often stepped in whenever he felt I was over my head with a customer.

He also always drove me home after my shifts, wanting to make sure I made it safe and sound.

I eventually gave up my small apartment and moved in with

Lucy, which was a good thing, especially once the baby arrived. She'd make sure we were on alternate shifts, so one of us was home with my sweet Alice, and the days when we had to both be on the floor, Darwin kept Alice by his side for me.

Alice, that's what I named my sweetheart. She was the most beautiful little being, almost like Little Bea here. She was the perfect baby, too, the most perfect. She rarely cried, she always slept the night, and she was content to just watch the world.

People would always be amazed that I would bring a baby into the diner, they thought the noises, the busyness would be too much for Alice to take in, but it never was. She loved going to the diner; I think she loved it more than just being at home with either me or Lucy.

Darwin loved her too. He kept asking me to move in with him, that I wouldn't need to work, that he'd take care of us. Looking back, maybe I should have taken that offer of his, but at the time, I enjoyed my freedom too much.

Being a waitress wasn't easy work, and you have to hustle for those tips. I had rules that both Lucy and Big Mike told me were necessary to survive.

Never sleep with a truck driver.

Never let them tip me too much.

Never go home with someone other than Darwin, Lucy or Big Mike.

I only ever broke those rules once. Once was all it took, too.

There was this trucker named Bruce. He was a mean SOB. He had the body of a wrestler, the temperament of a monster and he never liked being told no.

His route would bring him into the diner twice a week. Lucy always made sure she put him at a table other than mine. Always. Everyone warned me about him, and I knew to stay off the floor as much as I could when he was around.

Then the perfect storm hit. The weather outside was miserable, which meant the diner was overcrowded. Lucy had to call everyone in to help cover the tables, and somehow I had Bruce sitting at my table. I pretended that it didn't matter, that he didn't scare me, but he'd caught wind somehow and used it to his advantage.

He lingered, long past the storm, but not past my shift. God, I wish he'd left before my shift was up. How different my life might have been if he had.

He waited until Darwin was distracted and Lucy was in the back. I'd just finished refilling his coffee cup for the fourth or fifth time when he grabbed my wrist and pulled me close to him.

"I think it's time you and I got acquainted." He put down a fifty-dollar bill and said that I could keep the change.

"That's too much. I'll be right back." I struggled to free myself, and looking back, I wished I'd poured the coffee in the pot I held down on his lap.

"I don't want no change. I just want you." He stood, grabbed the coffee pot from my hand, and slammed it down on the table. He then took the fifty and stuffed it inside my bra. I can still remember the feel of his sticky fingers against my skin.

"I'm not for sale." I try to wrestle myself from his stronghold, but he won't let go of me. I look around, desperate for someone to notice I needed help, but no one was around. He started to drag me toward the door, and after yelling for Darwin, someone finally came to my rescue.

Big Mike.

He plowed out of the kitchen doors, his big body barreling toward us. Bruce never knew what hit him. Big Mike's beefy arms are like steel, and I've seen him knock out a few truck drivers who got too friendly with the staff.

As soon as I was free, I ran toward Alice and huddled there, my body shaking while I held her tight against me. I'd never been so scared before.

"I paid that bitch. I want my money's worth." Bruce's thick voice wrapped itself around me, and I turned, not wanting to see him, hoping he wouldn't notice me.

"Get out of here, and if you know what's good for you, you won't come back." Big Mike used his dangerous voice, the one that scared the hell of out anyone who heard it.

It took forever for me to calm down. I sat in the back, with Alice, for the longest time. I'd given Darwin the fifty dollars from Bruce. I wanted nothing to do with it.

By the time I was off shift, I'd calmed down and was fine. I went back on the floor after about an hour and acted as if nothing had happened, but I kept my eye out on the lot outside, making sure Bruce didn't come back.

I told Darwin I'd meet him in his truck, which was parked out back. This is what I did most nights…walked out of the back of the kitchen, down three steps, took maybe ten more steps, and I was there, at Darwin's truck.

He parks so close to the diner that I never feel like I'm in danger.

That night, I should have been on the lookout. I should have known better.

Alice was hungry and fussy, her little cries had me rushing to the truck, so I could feed her. Darwin had locked the door, and I struggled to get the key out of my pocket while holding the bassinet that Alice laid in.

All of a sudden, there was a thick, beefy hand on my shoulder, and I was twisted around. Before I could even make a sound, I was pushed against the truck. Everything I'd held onto tossed from my grasp, including Alice. All I remember was trying to reach out to grab hold of the handle of her bassinet while a cocked fist was coming toward my face.

I don't remember anything after that.

I don't remember apparently being held up in Bruce's stronghold as he raped me against that truck.

I don't remember Darwin coming out and pulling a gun on Bruce.

I certainly don't remember the sound of the shot that killed him.

Or, how my daughter looked when Darwin retrieved her from where Bruce had tossed her bassinet.

I'm so glad I don't remember that.

He'd killed her. That monster. When he swiped her from my

148

hand, when the bed that was supposed to keep her safe was flung across the yard, she landed face first on the dirt.

I was told she died immediately.

I was told there was nothing I could have done.

I was told that eventually, my heart would heal, and I could have more babies.

That's something no one should ever tell another parent. Never tell someone who grieves that their heart will heal. Never suggest having another baby could replace the one they lost.

That was a cruelty I didn't deserve.

CHAPTER
SIX

MARY TO JACK

I didn't know about Alice's death until I was in the hospital.

When Bruce hit me, he hit me good, and I was out for about three hours.

The nurses all told me it was a blessing.

I consider it a curse.

I never got to say goodbye to Alice.

They never let me see her, can you imagine?

Things were so different back then.

If car seats were mandatory, maybe she would have been safe, but back then, the safety of our little ones wasn't all that...important. It's sad, don't you think? I was lucky to have a bassinet to carry her in, but I certainly never strapped her in with a seat belt.

Parents today, they take such good care of their children. Back then, we had no idea that this was something we should have done. My Momma, she held her babies in the car when Daddy drove, and if she was the one driving, I was the one holding the youngest baby. I thought I was doing well to have something for Alice to lay in.

It wasn't enough, though.

They should have let me see her.

Maybe then things would have been different. I might have said goodbye. I might have had some closure.

But as it was - one minute she was with me, and we were going to go home and then next I'm being told she was dead.

It's safe to say this was the catalyst for what happened next.

Jack, a mother should always have the chance to say goodbye, don't you think?

I made sure that I said goodbye to all my children downstairs...I know I'm leaving a hole in their hearts, I know that it's going to be hard for them to continue without me, but that's the way of life, isn't it?

A child says goodbye to their parent and learns to move on... it's the natural progression of life. They'll be okay, I know it. With the nurses down there and Ike...and maybe even you?

Will you check in on them for me, Jack? Not all the time, just a few times, making sure they're okay? For me?

Thank you. That eases my heart. You're a good man Jack, a really good man.

CHAPTER
SEVEN

MARY

Mental health wasn't something everyone was on the lookout for, not for regular people.

I would wander through the hospital halls, always making my way toward the floor where all the newborn babies were. Whenever I was found hovering over a baby, the nurses just told the parents I was grieving my own baby's loss, and everyone gave me those sympathetic glances.

A few even let me hold their babies for a while.

I remember there was one baby; all she did was cry.

Cry and cry and cry, and you could see the new mom was exhausted and barely holding on.

It was hard to listen to the little thing, my heart broke, and my breast milk wouldn't stop. I snuck in once, in the middle of the night, while the woman slept and held that baby, even fed her with my own breast milk. Tears fell from my face as I held that precious little bundle, and I knew…I just knew that I wasn't done being a mom and that this baby, she needed me.

No one stopped me when I walked out of that room with her in my arms.

No one questioned me when I left the hospital, still holding her.

I walked from the hospital to Lucy's house and crawled into bed, making sure to hold the baby tight in my arms.

She reminded me so much of Alice. A little younger, but there was a look in her eyes that called to me. She recognized me, I just knew it.

The amazing thing was…while I could hear the cries from this sweet thing all the time in the hospital, she never cried when she was with me.

She was the perfect angel.

I still remember how she would look at me…so trusting, with the recognition of an old soul.

When I close my eyes, I can picture her still, you know?

I can picture them all when I try. But Alice…my Alice is the one that is always there, with me, like a presence, a ghost, I guess. I can't wait till I close my eyes here and open them to see her standing there, waiting for me, because I know she is.

My little girl has always been waiting for me.

Lucy was a heavy sleeper and didn't hear me when I came in or packed my things. I didn't have much, basically enough to fill a suitcase and a diaper bag. I grabbed a box for the baby to sleep in too, on my way out.

I put everything in the car that I rarely drove - I hated driving - and couldn't believe that I managed to leave without Lucy waking.

The baby, she was an absolute doll.

When I drove out of town, I didn't look back, not once. I didn't think about what I was doing or where I was going, or even how I was feeling.

I remember my body feeling so bruised. The side of my face where Bruce had hit me, it was swollen and badly bruised and hurt like crazy. I didn't let myself think about it, though, not about the pain or what happened to me or my sweet Alice.

In fact, at that moment, Alice was still very much alive and was sleeping in the little bed I'd fashioned out of a box.

I don't remember how long I drove or even the towns I drove through. I slept in the vehicle, stopped in little towns for some food and diapers, and continued to head west.

All I wanted was to head to the ocean, something I've always wanted to see.

I know what you're thinking: this baby became a replacement for the one I lost.

You're probably right. I even called her Baby Alice.

Baby Alice and I, those were the best days for us. I'd pull over when she got fussy, fed her, sang to her, take her for walks to stretch our legs.

It took us almost a week to hit the shoreline. It was a little town on the coast, with a gas station, a diner, a grocery store, and a few other buildings. It had the look of a sleepy town, and it was perfect. I looked at the message board at the gas station and saw a Help Wanted ad for a receptionist at an office downtown.

Everything went my way. Not only did I get the job, but I was able to rent out a room at a boarding house, and it came with free child care. The woman who owned the boarding house was an old grandmother, and I couldn't have asked for a better caregiver for Alice.

Life was idyllic for the first six months. Alice and I were doing fine; we had a comfortable room to live in, I made money in a safe environment, and Baby Alice was healthy and growing.

Then the nightmares started happening. I don't remember what brought them on. Still, I'd wake up screaming for my baby, and nothing could soothe me, not even holding Baby Alice in my arms.

In my dreams, I was at my daughter's graveside, throwing dirt on her tiny little coffin, and I was all alone. The nightmares became a nightly occurrence, to the point where whenever Baby Alice was out of my sight, I thought for sure she was dead.

I even started bringing her to work with me, having her sit on the floor beside my chair, because I couldn't bear to be without her.

Then one day, Baby Alice started to cough. It reminded me of that croupy-type cough, the barking seal one. Nothing I did helped her...not the long walks in the middle of the night when the cool air was supposed to help her, or even sitting in the bathroom with the shower going.

I became so scared, so worried, no matter what people told me, no matter how many times I took her to the local doctor...she just wouldn't stop coughing.

I wasn't a stranger when it came to croup - my brothers and sisters often had it when they were little, but a seed of fear took root inside my soul that no matter how much I loved her, no matter what I did to protect her, my baby was going to die.

So I did the only thing I knew to do.

One night, I filled my car with everything I owned and drove toward the nearest city. Alice had graduated to a larger bassinet that she slept in, given to me by my landlady.

When I arrived at the hospital, I sat in the parking lot for the longest time, unable to do what I knew needed to be done. If I wanted to save my baby, I needed to give her up if I wanted her to live.

I wrote a note, asking that they return her to the hospital that I took her from, that I realize I couldn't take care of her anymore and that I was sorry.

I left her on the sidewalk, close to the entrance, and I parked far enough away that no one would notice me but that I could watch over her and make sure someone found her.

Sure enough, two minutes after I left, someone walked out the doors and spied her. They looked around, then bent down and picked up the box.

As soon as they walked into the hospital with her, I let the tears flow as I drove away.

CHAPTER
EIGHT

MARY TO JACK

Losing a child is hard, Jack.

Grief is an ugly monster, one with tentacles that cling on and never let go.

Everyone deals with grief differently.

Leaving that sweet baby at the hospital almost destroyed me. I drove to the water, parked my car, and walked into the water, with the intent to drown my sorrows until I stopped breathing.

For over six months, I lived in a make-belief bubble, one that had me as the perfect mother, with the perfect child, and nothing could go wrong.

I refused to see the difference between my baby and the one I took. In my heart, she was Alice, my Alice, and it wasn't until the nightmares and then her getting sick that I realized what I'd done.

Did I feel bad? Absolutely.

I could have turned myself in, but I thought my death would be intonement enough. I was wrong.

I remember when I saw her again, in the courtroom. A few of my babies were there, along with their parents. Some spoke out against me, sharing the harm I caused them, the emotional trauma.

No one spoke about my trauma, though.

No one talked about what it was like for me to lose a child as I did -

not being able to say goodbye. No one thought of what that does to a woman, to a mother.

Postpartum depression or psychosis wasn't a thing back then. I was just a monster — a woman to be feared.

But that Alice, that sweet, beautiful Alice, she wrote me a letter. I'm not sure if that was ever revealed. She told me she forgave me, that she believes I loved her as best as I could and that she bore no ill will toward me.

Her parents raised her to be a good Christian girl, I could tell. She even said she'd be praying for me. I never heard from her again, but then, I never expected to.

Her name was Isabelle. Isn't that a beautiful name? But then, at the time, she was just Baby Alice to me.

It's easy for me to say now that I understand what drove me to take that sweet little girl from her sleeping mother. I was hurting, and I saw a need and a way to heal my broken heart.

I didn't understand what I did at the time. I honestly believe that. I was a mother in need of a baby, and when I heard those cries, I thought she was a baby in need of a loving mother.

I loved her, Jack.

I loved that sweet baby and didn't harm her at all.

Newborns, all they need is love, and that's what I gave her. Unconditional love. As far as she knew, I was her mother, and she was my daughter.

I still consider her my daughter, even though I know I've had to share her with someone else all these years.

CHAPTER
NINE

MARY

The one thing about our country, it's easy to get lost in the crowd if you want to.

Well, maybe not nowadays, I suppose, but back then, there wasn't anything such as the internet or cell phones or facial recognition.

I landed in a different city, in Wyoming, of all places and created a new life for myself.

I landed a new job easily enough and found another place to rent with no issues. I kept my head down and barely existed as I tried to heal my wounded soul.

In small towns, everyone knows who you are or who you pretend to be. In the city, no one cares, and it's easy to turn a blind eye.

After work, I used to walk through a local park, find a bench and sit for an hour or so while reading a book.

I hated going back to my empty one room apartment where the echoes of a baby's laughter would ring in my ears non-stop. At the park, even if I wasn't living life, I was a part of it, watching others live around me while I merely existed.

I was so lonely.

I should have gone back home to my parents, but that would have been admitting defeat and that my parents were right after all. I had too much pride to do that.

I used to pray that God would give me another baby.

I didn't care how, I didn't care if I had to sleep with a stranger...I just needed a baby. I was an empty shell, living a life without a goal. I was a living ghost and unsure why I was here if not to be a mother to a child who needed to be loved.

And yet, that's exactly what I was. A mother without a child. An empty shell. A living ghost.

I could have drowned my sorrows in alcohol. I should have drowned myself in the ocean. I could have done a number of things, and yet I did nothing, just waited for life to happen.

So I sat at the park.

Little by little, I noticed myself venturing closer to the play area, where the mothers would sit and chat while their kids played. Heading to the park was a break for most of the mothers, it seemed like. They didn't play with their kids, push them on the swings or build sandcastles...no, they sat with others who were just as exhausted as they were. I didn't judge them, and I still don't. Society today is so quick to condemn others, throw stones, and project our own fears onto others.

Things were different back then. More relaxed, I guess.

I remember several instances when mothers would leave their babies in the strollers, walk away to talk to another parent or deal with their crying child, and never thought twice about it. Now we have helicopter parents, but back then, that was unheard of.

I can't tell you the number of times I'd have someone ask me to keep an eye on their child while they walked away - me, a complete stranger. Of course, I always said yes. Why wouldn't I?

That's basically how I found my next child. I was sitting in the park, it was a beautiful Sunday morning, and I got immersed in a book. I blocked out most of the sounds around me, from the birds, traffic, barking dogs, and whatnot. But there was one sound I couldn't ignore...and that was of a crying baby.

I tried, I really did. I couldn't pinpoint where the sound was coming from at first, but it was persistent, and the longer it continued, the weaker it sounded.

I remember walking around, trying to find this crying baby, but I couldn't find it. Not at first. I thought maybe someone was playing a trick on me, or perhaps this was all a dream, and then I came to a shaded area where there were trees and shrubs, and shoved in between two bushes was a stroller.

A stroller!

That poor little baby boy, his face was blotted and red, and by the time I found him, he'd exhausted himself with his cries. There was no one around, no one. He'd been abandoned. There was a bag of washable diapers, some formula, and a teddy bear, but that was it. No note, no hint of who he was, his name, his parents' name...nothing.

I could have taken him to a hospital or even to a police station, but I didn't do either of those things.

He was a gift from God. A gift for me, and who was I to turn this away. God knew I needed a baby, that I ached for a child to love, that I was a shadow of a person at that moment, and he was the one thing that could breathe life into me.

I brought him home. He was the tiniest of beings and so thin. I wasn't sure he'd survive that first night. I held him close, skin to skin, for the longest time, singing softly, touching his skin, letting him know he wasn't alone and never would be again.

I called in sick the next day. And then the rest of the week...I just couldn't leave him. After the first few days, he seemed to settle in, like he knew he was finally safe. I could only imagine what his life must have been like before I found him...and he only had to be a month or two old.

All that little boy needed was love. Love and a sense of safety, and that's exactly what I gave him.

Right from the beginning, I knew he wasn't mine to keep, but he was mine to save, and so that's just what I did.

He didn't have a name right away, and to be honest, I didn't know what to call him other than my sweet little boy. In the end, I gave him my Daddy's name - Walter Michael and called him Willy.

Willy had the sweetest of smiles, the loudest laughs, and wise owl eyes. After finding him in the park, he never cried hard, he just mewed. I think he cried all the tears he had that day, knowing he'd been abandoned, and it exhausted him.

A young couple lived across the hallway from me, and the young woman stayed home with her toddler. She ended up babysitting for me while I worked. They were the most adorable couple I'd ever seen. He was a hard working man who dotted on his wife. She was the sweetest, most docile person I'd ever met, and all she wanted was to make her husband happy.

One day, while we shared a cup of tea, she confided that she couldn't have any more children and was simply heartbroken over the news. She'd had several miscarriages, and her doctor recently told her to be happy with just having one child.

I felt for her. I shared with her that I had lost a child and that little Willy was my saving grace. We bonded then and there, and I watched as she continued to fall in love with my sweet little boy. More and more, she offered to watch him, offered to take him on the weekends if I needed to run to the store...and I started to think that maybe God gave me him so I could give him to her.

I didn't rush anything. I couldn't. I'd grown to love the little man even though I knew he wasn't mine to keep. I wasn't ready to say goodbye, though...even though I knew eventually I'd have to.

One day, I let it slip that William wasn't mine, not truly. I explained how I'd found him, how I brought him home and took care of him. She was shocked, and I don't blame her. She asked why I didn't take him to the hospital or report him to the police. That's when I told her the truth about Alice. I saw it in her eyes, the lack of judgment, the full understanding. I also saw how she looked at Willy...with a longing, a desire stronger than my own.

I asked her if she would like to keep William, as her own. At first, she said no. I knew she wanted to say yes.

So I made it easy for her. I decided it was time for me to leave, to move to someplace new. I didn't know where, but I knew this was the right thing to do. I gave my notice for my job, told my landlord I'd be leaving, and one morning, I packed up everything I had for William into a diaper bag and handed it to my sweet neighbor.

I told her I had to leave for a family emergency, a lie, and we both seemed to know it. I asked her if she would take care of William for me, love him like her own. We shed a few tears, gave each other a few hugs, and by the time I placed him in her arms, I could barely see through the tears.

Walking away was so hard. So very, very hard.

I never heard from her or William again. Not during my trial, not after either. I'm okay with that. I know she loved him and that he was okay. I wouldn't have left him with her otherwise.

CHAPTER
TEN

MARY TO JACK

You look surprised about that one - I guess that was my secret, one I've never shared before. Now that I think about it, no one ever knew about William, did they?

All my children came to me at the exact time I was needed. They were blessings from God. I honestly believe that, Jack.

Why else would he have directed me their way? Why else would I have found them all like I did?

I never actively sought out my little ones.

I never woke up one morning intending to find a child to call my own. I know that's what they said I did, that I was on the hunt...but that was never true.

The children, they came to me. They all found me, one way or another.

I couldn't ignore them. I couldn't leave them. I couldn't turn my back on them.

Leaving a child's cry unanswered has never been part of my DNA.

Therapy has taught me that I could have saved the children in other ways, but back then, I did what I thought was best.

Every action I took from the moment I woke up in the hospital has been in reaction to losing my daughter like I did.

If I had been able to say goodbye, if I had been able to hold her, to rock her, to hold her close…maybe things would have been different.

But you can't look back on life and live on the 'what ifs'. That's not how life works.

If you live with regrets, then you're not truly living. You're reacting in order to not live with more regrets. Don't do that, Jack.

Wake up each day determined to be the best person you can be. Go to sleep each night knowing you did the absolute best you could and that it's too late to change actions you've already taken.

Determine to be absolute in your decisions, and you'll never experience a moment of regret.

Regret can destroy dreams, did you know that?

When all you do is focus on the things that went wrong in your life, you miss out on what could be happening, the good things. That's not a way to live. I tell my girls that downstairs all the time.

I don't regret any child that came into my life.

I don't regret loving them, taking care of them, making sure they were safe.

I don't live with regrets, nor should I.

That's the only way a person can live, Jack. Do you hear me? Do you understand?

I think you do.

Thank you for never judging me. I do appreciate that. I know there are those in this building who have. Some have hated me, misunderstanding who I am, and that's okay.

I'm no Mother Theresa, and that's plenty fine with me.

CHAPTER
ELEVEN

MARY

You obviously know about Katie, the baby I found locked in a car at a busy mall, right?

What you don't know is the whole story.

No one does. They just know what was in the news, and we all know that the news isn't always accurate. What you hear is worded to get a reaction. It's rarely the full truth, only hints, and tiny pieces.

It's why I hate listening to the news, even now. Every single story you hear, don't take it as truth. It's slanted toward a fact they want the public to believe. You always have to look beyond the words they are telling you and find the other side.

There is always another side.

I was painted as a deranged woman seeking a child to replace the one I'd lost. No child was safe while I was on the loose - I was a danger to every single parent with a child younger than one year.

They didn't tell you that I wasn't actively searching for a child to love and protect.

What they didn't say was how this child had found me. How

the parents of little Katie had left her, neglected her, and all I did was rescue her.

No. I was in the wrong. I was the monster. The neglectful mother had done absolutely nothing wrong, right?

Spare me.

I had just moved, again. By this time, I'd had four more children come into my life over the course of three years. Two girls and two boys, all neglected, all alone, all below the age of one, and all needing love.

I always knew they weren't mine to keep, just mine to love while I could.

I never seemed to stay in one place for very long, but each place I stayed, I found a child. I didn't actively search them out; they just appeared at the right time.

All four children I would leave at the nearest city hospital, where I wouldn't be seen. By this point, I'd crisscrossed the country and saw most of the things I'd only dreamed about. The ocean, the Grand Canyon, the lush mountains, and dry earth…we live in such a beautiful and diverse country. In the short amount of time that I lived outside of these walls, I saw more than most people do in their lifetimes.

More than my parents had, that's for sure.

Why did I move so much? Moving meant running. Running meant never having to face the utter sadness in my soul. I was always trying to make new memories, hoping that I wouldn't get lost in the past by focusing on the road ahead.

I stayed away from men for the main part. I had a few relationships and ended up pregnant twice, but my body rejected both pregnancies, and I had miscarriages even before I felt the flutter of the first movement.

I once had a counselor suggest that it was my body's way to telling me I was too broken and that I needed help. It's possible. My body has always had a rebellious spirit, I guess.

I could talk about those four babies that I found, but there was so much said about them during my trial, that I have nothing new to add. The mothers all condemned me, the fathers threatened to kill me, but no one ever talked about what happened for me to find these babies in the first place.

No one talked about how they'd been left alone, about the neglect from the parents themselves...no, I was the monster.

You know, I think that's what I'll be most thankful for when I finally close my eyes for good. There will be no more name calling other than the one name I hold most dear...Mother.

I can't wait to see Alice again.

I'd like to tell you about the baby I found at the mall.

I had just moved and this time to another small town in the middle of nowhere. I noticed several help-wanted signs in different business windows and decided to try my luck. The first place I walked into was an antique shop run by an older man. He hired me on the spot, said I seemed sensible enough. When I'd asked if there were any places close by to rent, he said he had owned the apartment above the shop, and it was empty if I wanted it. I had to agree to both open and close the shop daily and promise to be a respectable tenant that didn't have men coming and going.

Considering I didn't know anyone, I didn't see that being a problem.

That was probably the easiest job I'd ever had, if I were being honest. I cleaned, I organized, I kept an old man company. I had two days off during the week and a few hours during the day to myself as well. It was perfect.

Weekends were the busiest in the shop, with many day-trippers coming in, browsing and walking out with items they didn't know they wanted. It turns out that I was good at selling old things and I thought that maybe, just maybe, I could be happy there.

The old man had no living family, no one to pass on the shop to, so he trained me to take over. He slowly started to teach me about what it took to run the shop, how to find items of value, how to appraise. There was a lot to learn, but I threw myself into it. It was a...welcome respite, I guess you could say.

I'd settled my heart that I would start a new life here, in this town, and that I would accept the death of the dream to be a mother again. I never sought out the children I found, but I was always open to them finding me. I realized that if I wanted to settle, I had to close myself to their voices to their cries and needs if I wanted to stop running.

It was a hard decision, but I was willing to make it.

Until the decision was taken from me, I had no choice but to answer the cry of a baby in need.

CHAPTER
TWELVE

MARY TO JACK

I was serious, Jack, when I said I was willing to close myself off to their cries of need.

All I'd done was run from my grief, and if I ever wanted to heal, it was time to stop running. I knew that.

Working with that old man, he was exactly what I needed. He'd lost everyone in his life - his wife, his two sons, and even a daughter. He understood what it was to be a father without a child. He said he recognized that pain in my eyes, which is why he hired me that day.

He told me something I've never forgotten.

If you're grieving, you need to let that grief sweep over you, wash over you, as if you were a pebble of sand adrift along the shoreline. Eventually, the strength of the water will pull you in until you are surrounded, and the very grief you thought was drowning you is, instead, supporting you.

I stopped fighting and instead surrendered.

It's incredible what surrendering does to a person. There's a freedom in it, Jack. A freedom that you never expect.

Did I ever look back and regret what I'd done? Why would you ask such a question? Of course not. Do you honestly believe I'd ever harm a child? That I would actively seek out a baby that was being loved and protected?

Have you not heard a single thing I said? Honestly, Jack, I'm surprised at you.

The children all came to me.

Why? I think because they knew I would help them.

Actually, I think Alice sent them to me. No - I believe she did. She's always watched out for me, even while I've been in here. She still brought the children to me, the children in spirit, who needed a mother's love. The ones downstairs needed a mother's love to help heal them, and that's what I tried to do.

Every child I found: I saved, I loved, and then I returned.

I never kept a single one.

No, I didn't return them to their parents directly, because I don't believe they deserved to have their children back. That was up to the authorities, and apparently, they thought otherwise. I should have found families for them, as I did with William.

I never felt the need to keep any of the children, not until Katie.

I'd like to tell you about her now if that's okay. And then...then I think I'd like to fall asleep for the last time. Will you help me with that, Jack?

Thank you.

CHAPTER
THIRTEEN

MARY

I remember that day as if it were just last year. It was a Wednesday, and I decided to take a drive and head to a mall.

Back then, that was a big outing. I'd given myself the whole day to walk through the mall, explore the different stores, even get food from the food court. I'd been saving up, ready to buy myself some new clothes and shoes, something I rarely did.

I usually would buy from second-hand stores or the sales rack at Woolworth. Is that store even around anymore?

I parked toward the back end of the already packed parking lot and headed in. I preferred to park far from others, so no one would ding my car. It was a junk piece, but it was the only thing I had, and I treated it like it was gold.

The mall was crazy inside, and I remember feeling extremely overwhelmed with all the store options. I think I lasted for maybe an hour and a half before I grabbed lunch from the food court and took it outside to eat. There was a crowd at the front door, and I watched as an ambulance pulled away.

There were way too many people milling around the entrance, so I went back to my car and contemplated just calling it a day and heading home.

When I'd first arrived, I was the only car in that whole section.

Wouldn't you figure, someone had to park right next time to me?

My initial response was to be annoyed; I mean, there were so many parking spots around us, why select the one right beside me? But my attention was grabbed by the slight cry that came through a barely opened passenger window.

I was the right person at the right time for this little soul.

It was a hot day. Too hot to leave a baby all alone in a vehicle. The little thing was just laying there, on the seat, a blanket beneath it to protect it, and a bottle at its side, one that it couldn't even reach.

Someone abandoned what looked like a two-month-old baby.

If that happened today, it would be one of the worst things one could do, right? Police would be called, the window would be broken to get in, and that child would be given to social services, no questions asked.

Back then...no one probably would have thought twice about needing to rescue that baby except for me.

I stayed for about an hour, ate my lunch, and watched over the baby.

It had stopped crying, seemed to be sleeping, and there was a bit of a breeze that I hoped it wasn't getting too hot. I did manage to get into the car, thanks to that open window. It took me a bit, though, but it was a good thing I did.

I know when a baby isn't doing well. By the time I held the little girl in my arms, she was so lethargic that my first instinct was to take her to the doctor. Rather than panic, I gave it some time.

I stayed for another hour, sitting in the shade beneath a tree, and held that precious little bundle. By the time she'd drank her bottle, she was doing better, but I couldn't in good conscious leave her. I mean...it had been two hours already.

Yes, back then, no one thought anything about leaving children in a vehicle while you ran errands. Abductions didn't happen as they do now. But two hours? No, that wasn't okay.

So I did the only thing I could. I brought that sweet baby home with me.

Of course, I did.

I told my boss that it was my sister's baby and I was taking care of her for a little while. He wasn't all that pleased until I promised the baby wouldn't get in the way. He let me use one of the cribs we had back in the storage area, and I went and bought some clothes from one of the stores in town.

I felt no remorse for taking little Katie. None whatsoever. She was another baby that was brought into my life because of someone else neglect.

Katie stayed with me the longest. Watching her grow was the best experience of my life. When she took her first steps to me, I cried as any proud parent would…but for more reasons than most. This was a first for me.

Katie and I experienced a lot of firsts together, actually…first crawl, the first step, first time drinking from a real cup, the first word, then sentence…she was the first child I'd really watched grow up.

Every other baby I knew wasn't mine to keep. It was different with Katie. Katie became my own, my forever daughter, and when I thought about my future, it was all focused around her.

For the longest time, no one ever asked about Katie; they seemed to believe my lie that she was my niece. When I started calling her my daughter, I had to backtrack a little, pretend my sister had died and there was no one else.

Everyone bought the lie. I even started to believe the lies. It's amazing the things we can get away with when we believe the lies we tell.

Life was perfect for us, and the future seemed so promising.

Until someone from my past unexpectantly came to town and tore my life to pieces. That was the beginning of the end for me.

CHAPTER
FOURTEEN

MARY TO JACK

When you live a lie, you have to be prepared to fully embrace your truth.

Have you ever had to adopt a truth you knew to be a lie, Jack?

We all lie.

Oh, come on, Jack. You know what I'm talking about: those little lies that we want others to believe to be the truth. You would call them little white lies, but they're lies all the same.

They're not always life-altering things.

Sometimes, it's telling someone they have the most beautiful baby you've ever seen. Or pretending to be okay when in fact, you're a mess inside. It can even be when you say I love you when really you hate the person.

I fully expected people to believe my lie because I believed it with my whole being. Katie was mine. Just because I didn't give birth to her didn't matter, not to me.

I see you understand me, Jack. I appreciate that, I really do. As a caregiver yourself, I knew you'd understand. You've never been one to judge me, and I appreciate that from you.

I know you are familiar with the rest of the story - how the authorities learned about Katie was national news.

Can I tell you the real story? Not the one everyone believes is the truth?

It would be nice to confide it to one person at least.

I was betrayed by family. After not seeing my family for over a decade, my youngest sister, the youngest of them all, came to town, quite by accident.

When she left, she took my daughter with her.

CHAPTER
FIFTEEN

MARY

It was easier to stay away from my family than it was to keep in touch.

I would send Christmas and birthday cards every year, call Mom every few months and find out how everyone was doing, but I never went home.

There was nothing there for me.

The day my youngest sibling, Theresa showed up in the antique shop, I should have known nothing good would come of it.

I should have been excited to see her, right?

I didn't know Theresa all that much, we had never gotten too close, which made sense because I left shortly after she'd been born.

Why she landed in my town, in my shop, I was shocked. I didn't recognize her at first, but she knew who I was right away.

I pretended to be happy to see her, thrilled that she managed to find me - because finding me was her goal. She saved my address from one of the birthday cards I'd sent home, and rather than call and see if she could come to stay with me, she decided to just see what happened.

A classic baby of the family move, right?

I welcomed Theresa to my humble home. She slept on my couch, saying it was better than sleeping in the backseat of her car, and I believed her. She took care of Katie for me without hesitation, which was nice.

It felt different having a roommate, odd to not have my own space after so many years. At first, I thought maybe she'd stay for a week or two, but that turned into a month, then two, then three.

As expected, we had a lot of long talks…and eventually, we settled into a pattern of sorts. I'll even admit that it was nice to have someone with me, to not be so alone…although I never admitted that to her.

When she met Katie, she was surprised, to say the least. I hadn't told anyone in my family about Katie, or any other babies, truth be told. They all knew about Alice and how she'd died, but all the others, I never breathed a word.

My boss was surprised to meet Theresa. The truth I'd told him had been one I'd carefully assembled…I never told him I came from a large family. He only ever knew about the sister I said had died.

Thankfully, Theresa played along when he offered his condolences.

I played off the fact he was older and often forgot things. She believed me, and why wouldn't she?

Eventually, I moved Katie into my room, and we fixed up that bedroom for Theresa. I'd come to grips that she was here with me for good, and when I told my parents, they were more than happy to know she'd landed in a safe place.

Theresa was a talker. She had so many questions for me and never took my silence as an answer. She wanted to know about my life, every aspect of it, every minute detail of what I'd done since leaving home. After being alone for so long, I'll be honest, it was really nice to have someone to talk to.

I'd forgotten how nice it was to have someone you could call a friend. If there's anyone you should be able to trust, it's family, right?

I see that smirk of yours, Jack. You know where I'm going with this, don't you?

Theresa stayed with me for six months.

That's six months where I learned to relax around her, where I trusted her with Katie, where I basically shared my heart with her.

In those six months, Theresa continued to ask me about Katie - who was her father, why wasn't he around, why did I never tell Mom and Dad...so many questions.

I told her what I could, but it never seemed to be enough.

Her curiosity should have had me on guard. What happened next was my own fault. I'll acknowledge that.

Then one day, I hear the slam of the back door, with Theresa running into the shop with a small box in her hands.

My heart dropped. Thankfully there was no one in the shop.

I couldn't move. I literally felt my feet cement into the floor, that's how heavy my body became.

She set the box on the counter between us and never said a word, but she didn't have to. It was all there in her eyes.

My hands trembled as I opened the box, the box that I'd hidden away at the back of my closet, the box that I didn't let myself look at too often. The box that held all my secrets.

One by one, I took out the polaroids of all my babies. I couldn't stop the smile that graced my face, despite the horror on Theresa's. On each, I'd written the name, the date, and the location where my babies had found me.

She asked if these were children I'd taken care of. I said yes.

She asked if these were children I'd taken care of as part of a job. I said no.

I told her these were all my children. Children I'd saved, loved as if they were my own. I thought she understood; she said she understood...

Then a customer walked in, and our conversation stopped.

Theresa gathered the photos, replaced them in the box, and calmly said we would talk tonight after closing.

For the rest of my shift, I was a nervous wreck. I broke a

teacup while dusting, I spilled the mop bucket all over the floor when emptying it, and I tripped on the stairs as I climbed up to the apartment.

I was nervous. Scared. Worried, Theresa wouldn't understand.

We waited until Katie was asleep before we settled on the couch, and I told her everything.

I told her...I didn't confess. I want to be clear on that distinction.

I had nothing to confess to. I never did anything wrong. Each child came to me, found me, and I took care of them.

When she asked about Katie and how I found her, I told her the honest truth. I didn't hide anything from her because I didn't feel I needed to.

I'll admit, it was lovely to finally share my secrets with someone else, someone who understood...because Theresa said she did. We hugged. She told me she loved me. She said that I'd always been someone she looked up to, admired for leaving the family and living an independent life like I was.

When I went to sleep that night, I had no idea how much my life was about to change.

I had a dream that night, one that was so vivid, I still remember it. Theresa and I...we rescued babies together. We were a team, and I remember waking up so happy.

I should have clued in when I noticed the empty crib.

I started to feel nervous when I walked out of the bedroom, and the apartment was empty. I wanted to believe that Theresa had taken Katie on a walk.

Except, when I looked in her bedroom, the closet door was open and it was empty. Also missing was Katie's diaper bag.

I ran down the stairs and out to the parking lot. Her car was gone.

She was gone, and she took my daughter with her.

I can't tell you the strength of the panic I felt at that moment.

I wanted to die. Oh God, I was so ready to die.

On the counter by the coffee pot was a note.

I'm righting your wrong. You need help.

I have no idea how long it took for the police to arrive, but I was ready. I showered and dressed and waited on the couch. I had the box in front of me, along with any small items I'd kept to remind me of the children.

The rest…the rest everyone knows.

The local woman who rescued Katie from her kidnapper, as the newspapers claimed, was my sister.

Theresa took Katie to the local police station and repeated the story I'd told her. They reunited Katie with her parents, and Theresa had been there to watch the reunion. Later, she told me when she came to see me in prison, about the parents, how they couldn't stop crying when they found their daughter.

She told me I'd been wrong, that I'd assumed I rescued Katie when the reality was, I stole her from parents who loved her, who had been searching for over a year for her.

That day, when I waited for two hours for someone to arrive, the reason no one did was that the mom had run into her work for a quick second to hand over keys and had passed out. She was the one being hauled away via ambulance when I'd left to eat my lunch.

No one knew she'd left her daughter in the car, not until hours later when her husband had been notified and went to retrieve their daughter…only to find an empty vehicle.

Knowing the whole story didn't change anything for me.

That woman should have taken her daughter with her into the mall, not left her in the car - bottom line.

Katie's real name was Brittany.

Yes, I said was.

Unfortunately, Brittany died a few years later. When I found out, I sobbed as if my heart had just broken in two. These bags you see under my eyes, it's because I cried so hard for that sweet little girl that it left these pockets.

If I'd known that night would have been my last with her, there's so much I would have told her.

Just like I wish I'd had the chance to say goodbye to my Alice.

Sometimes we never get the chance to properly say goodbye to someone. That's just how life plays out, I guess.

CHAPTER
SIXTEEN

MARY TO JACK

Remember at the beginning, I told you that I met one of the mothers here in the Asylum?

It was Brittany's mother. Her name was Allison, and she was a fragile thing.

I don't think Allison ever knew who I was or that I was here. If she did, she didn't seem to care.

I think the nurses kept us separated, just in case. Not that I ever worried Allison would harm me. No, it was the other way around, I'm sure. The nurses kept us separated so I wouldn't hurt Allison.

Allison came to be at the Asylum because she couldn't be trusted around her children. Turns out my sweet Katie, or Brittany as she was called, had a baby sister.

Allison tried to drown both girls in the bathtub. She was successful with my sweet girl.

The little baby survived but, from what I heard, had brain damage. She died a few years after Allison came here.

Allison barely lived when she was here. She rarely spoke, shuffled her feet all the time, and always had to hold on to someone's hand as she walked.

Her husband never came to visit. Not that I blame him.

Do I feel responsible for breaking Allison? Why do you assume I broke her? She had her daughter back for at least two years. My sister never mentioned there was something wrong with her.

So no. The answer is no, I don't take responsibility for Allison's emotional well-being.

No regrets, remember, Jack? I live with no regrets.

CHAPTER
SEVENTEEN

JACK

Mary fell asleep with me holding her hand.

I watched as she breathed her last breath, and I waited a few more minutes before taking the doll from her arms.

Mary's last words had been goodbye to her doll. I didn't want to take that from her.

When I left her room, I found Tonya sitting on the floor, tears rolling down her face. I helped her to her feet, and together we walked back to the desk.

"It never gets easy, saying goodbye, does it?" Tonya wipes her eyes with a tissue that Ike hands her.

"Did you listen in?" Ike sounds surprised, but I'd known she'd been there the whole time. I heard her little hiccups and sniffles on the other side of the door.

"When Jack takes a confession, you give him the space he needs. I thought I told you that." Ike is gruff, and I was about to interrupt him, but he gave his head a quick shake, so I stopped.

He's trying to teach Tonya a lesson, and I get that.

"Those confessions are for his ears alone. Did Mary ask you to stay? You didn't respect her last moments by listening in." He doesn't soften his voice, and it seems to be just what Tonya needs.

She stops crying, straightens her shoulders, and gives me an apology.

I give my head a deep nod and wait till she walks away.

"I knew she was there," I say.

He lifts his shoulder in a shrug. "Figured. Still, she knows better."

"It also wasn't a real confession. I didn't offer her a deal."

"Doesn't matter," Ike says, and he's right. It doesn't matter, and Tonya does know better.

"I hope Mary is surrounded by children," Ike says as he gets to his feet and clears his throat. "I hope Alice is there giving her a big hug and that her broken heart is finally healed."

I don't say anything as he heads toward Mary's room. I don't need to.

Mary was special. She deserved to be here; she was so broken, this was the only safe place for her to be.

I'm glad I got to know her, though.

I head into my office and pour myself a double of whatever is in my desk drawer. It won't be enough, but it'll tide me over till I get to the pub tonight.

I plan on getting piss drunk tonight and maybe, just maybe, shed a few tears when I'm alone.

CONFESSION BOOK #3

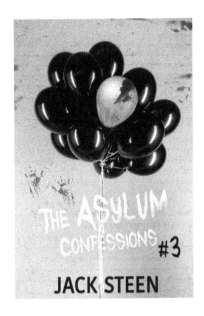

The Asylum Confessions: Book 3 - All About Love

The couples that kill together…well, they for sure don't stay together, right? These confessions deal with couples…

- One is a Preacher with a past.
- Another shouldn't be trusted.
- What's with farmers with buried secrets?
- And another who has a thing for soil and gardens.

CONFESSION BOOK #4

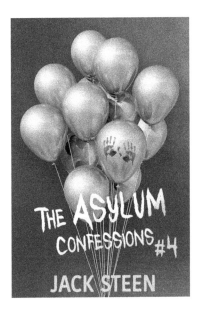

The Asylum Confessions: Book 4 - CULTS

Trust me on this…these confessions will take you on a wild ride:

- One thought she gave birth to the antichrist.
- Another was called the Candyman…any guess why?
- One grew up in a cult and believes he was the first of a 'pure' race.
- Then there's the guy who claims he was part of a secret test by the government and I've been waiting on his confession for a while!
- Finally, this one who loved Halloween and believed in all the rules. I sure you hope you didn't break any…

CONFESSION BOOK #5

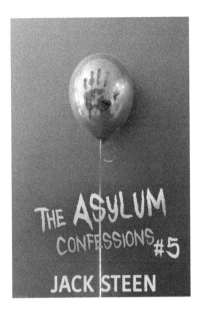

The Asylum Confessions: Book 5 - Fairytales

This book has confessions that remind me of the original Grimm brothers tales - you know, the good ones.

- Think Modern Day Sleeping Beauty – with a twist.
- One with a resemblance to Rapunzel that is kind of scary.
- One reminds me of Cinderella…with a thing for shoes.

CONFESSION BOOK #6

The Asylum Confessions: Book 6 - Happy Merry and All That

Christmas isn't always a merry thing for people. These confessions focus on the holiday theme and patients who:

- Likes to nibble on sugar cookies while watching his victim die
- Another likes to replace the jam in the thumbprint cookies with blood
- One patient has a thing about gingerbread cookies and revenge
- And then there's one - give her some candy cane shortbread cookies - after all she's been through, she deserves them.

MORE CONFESSION BOOKS?

Hell yes.

I've got notepads full of confessions.

If you want them, I'll make them available. The more you buy, the more beer I drink, so guess it's a win-win.

Head to my website and sign up - www.jacksteenbooks.com or CLICK HERE FOR NEWSLETTER

FINAL WORD

Listen…I could give a rats ass whether you believe me or not, whether you think these confessions are real..but let me say this:

When I say I won't tell you where I work, where I live or give the real names of my patients - there's one solid reason for it.

Some people think they know better and have 'opinions' about what I do.

I don't give two fucks about those opinions. I do care about the people around me though. When I put this first book out, I had no idea people would want to read it - and especially didn't think you'd want to read more of them.

I got cocky. I got comfortable. I've done too much and said too much on social media - which is my bad.

To make it 100% clear since some people can't wrap their heads around this: I have people who help me do the stuff needed to make these books available. Someone who helps with the audio. Someone who formats these things and puts them online for me. Someone who makes graphics. Someone who posts for me online (my words - they just copy and paste).

Every single person who helps me make these books available for you to read - they don't know who I am, not the real me. They have no idea where I live, work, or anything else. We communicate via email only.

Got that?

There are some real sick fucks out there.

I doubt you're one of them, so do me a favor? Stay safe. Behave. Join my newsletter or watch my website - I'll let you know when I have a new book out, but other than that...

Well, my original offer still stands: if you figure out who I am and want to join me for a beer, you know where I'll be.

Jack

Printed in the USA
CPSIA information can be obtained
at www.ICGtesting.com
CBHW060023160224
4391CB00011B/941

9 781987 877373